THE EDGE OF EVIL

GOOD TO THE LAST DEMON BOOK 2

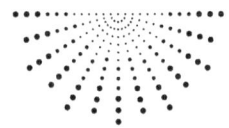

ROBYN PETERMAN

JOIN MY NEWSLETTER!

Copyright © 2022 by Robyn Peterman

All rights reserved.

No part of this book may be reproduced in any form or by any electronic or mechanical means, including information storage and retrieval systems, without written permission from the author, except for the use of brief quotations in a book review.

This book is a work of fiction. Names, characters, places, and incidents either are the product of the author's imagination or are used fictitiously. Any resemblance to actual persons, living or dead, businesses, companies, events, or locales is coincidental.

This book contains content that may not be suitable for young readers 17 and under.

Cover design by *Cookies Inc.*

Edited by *Kelli Collins*

ACKNOWLEDGMENTS

As The Edge of Evil is a spinoff of The Good To The Last Death Series. You don't have to have read the other series, but there are fun call outs for those who have. Candy Vargo makes a big appearance in this one.

I wrote The Facts of Midlife knowing I was going to spin Abaddon off into his own series.
And then I came up with the perfect heroine.

I promised myself a very long time ago that someday I would write a story about an actress and use some of my real life experiences…
That time has come. LOL
The names have been changed to protect the innocent and the guilty.

The situations have been slightly altered.
Clearly, I'm not a Demon—well not on a daily basis.
Cecily, our new and fabulous heroine, is a Demon.

So get ready for a wild, wild ride. I had a blast writing As The Underworld Turns and hope you love reading about Abaddon and Cecily.

As always, writing may be a solitary sport, but it takes a bunch of terrific people to get a book out into the world.

Renee — Thank you for my beautiful cover and for being the best badass critique partner in the world. TMB. LOL

Kelli — Your editing makes me look like a better writer. Thank you.

Wanda — You are the freaking bomb. Love you to the moon and back.

Heather, Nancy, Susan, Caroline and Wanda — Thank you for reading early and helping me find the booboos. You all rock.

My Readers — Thank you for loving the stories that come from my warped mind. It thrills me.

Steve, Henry and Audrey — Your love and support makes all of this so much more fun. I love you people endlessly.

DEDICATION

For my Kurt. You are my sunshine.

MORE IN THE GOOD TO THE LAST DEMON SERIES

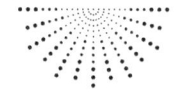

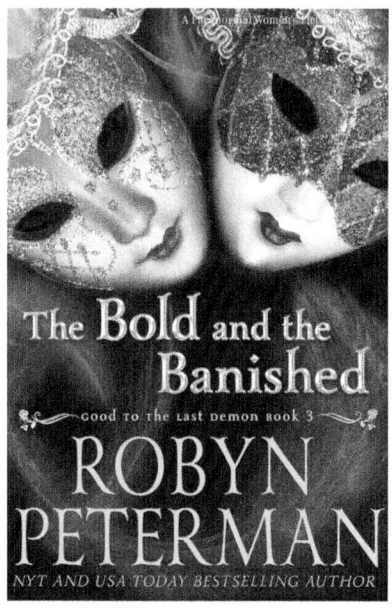

ORDER BOOK THREE NOW!

BOOK DESCRIPTION

THE EDGE OF EVIL

What happens in Vegas, *slays* in Vegas.

With a show to produce and my career as an actress on the line, I really don't have time to die—especially violently. However, while that might not be on my agenda, it seems to be on other's.

Awesome.

Instead of acting in my latest endeavor, I'm playing the real-life role of Reluctant Demon Who Has To Save The World—or at the very least, the hot hero.

Fine. I'm always up for a plot twist or a re-write.

Scene One— Save Abaddon from the evil clutches of the hideous Pandora.

Scene Two — Don't die.

Scene Three — Avoid Pandora like the plague. I understand she has an evil box…

Scene Four — Do not die.

Scene Five — Possibly meet my mom, the woman who abandoned me as a baby.

Scene Six — Do Not Freaking Die.

Scene Seven — Go back to my non-deadly life and win a damn Emmy for *Ass The World Turns*.

Even though I'm living on the edge of evil, half insanity, half upheaval, I'm a pro and the show must go on.

As the saying goes, a bad dress rehearsal means I don't get dismembered on opening night. Or something like that.

It's showtime, folks.

***The Good To The Last Demon Series is a spinoff of the Good To The Last Death Series.

CHAPTER ONE

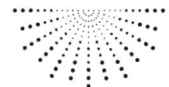

C̲o̲u̲l̲d̲ ̲m̲y̲ ̲l̲i̲f̲e̲ ̲g̲e̲t̲ ̲a̲n̲y̲ ̲s̲t̲r̲a̲n̲g̲e̲r̲?

I just admitted to Abaddon that I liked him and wanted to date. The dating scene had never been my forte. Sanity and self-preservation were lacking in my skill set, but he'd almost died for me. That was *huge*. I'd also kissed the Demon. It had been a damn good kiss—best of my forty years. Not to mention, I'd recently discovered I was also a Demon. My dead naked uncle was hanging around, and my other uncle was the Grim Reaper. Who could even make that up? I was in the process of making all my dreams come true by starring in my own TV show while trying to stay alive at the same time.

No. The answer was a definitive no. My life could not get any stranger… I hoped.

"Who rings a doorbell?" I asked no one as I walked through the house and made sure nothing looked as if otherworldly creatures—like myself—had been hanging out, electrocuting people, casting spells or bleeding all over the place.

Nope. Everything looked incredibly normal considering all

the crazy magical juju that had gone down. The mystery visitor couldn't be my dad or my brother. They had keys to my house. Uncle Joe was transparent and could float through walls. Ophelia and Rhoda, aka Nip Slip—my unwanted demonic protectors—could poof. Plus, they were out checking the perimeter for tears and evil Demons lurking around. The Grim Reaper and Daisy could poof too. I saw them do it when they'd left.

After all the time I'd lived here, I wasn't close with any of my neighbors. Everyone kept to themselves. LA was like that. Maybe it was a delivery… or a flaming asshole Demon stopping by to kill me.

"Shit," I muttered, pausing mid-step. "Would a flaming asshole ring the bell?"

The thought made my stomach cramp. If it was a flaming asshole, that meant there was a tear in the perimeter and that Nip Slip and Ophelia were probably dead.

I shook my head and inhaled deeply. I was being ridiculous. The two women had been chosen because of their power. Abaddon was not a dummy. And as much as I'd enjoyed electrocuting Ophelia, I certainly didn't want the *beewby* blonde dead. Plus, Abaddon would have to let a flaming asshole inside the perimeter. I was positive none of them were on the invite list.

"Coming," I called out as the bell kept ringing.

Peeking through the peephole, I laughed with an absurd amount of relief. What the heck was my agent Cher doing here at 8 PM? And why was she wielding one of my blowtorches?

"Cecily," Cher yelled. "Let me in. Shit's not right."

My relief turned to panic at her words. Yanking the door open, I grabbed Cher by the collar of her way-too-tight pink power suit and pulled her into the house. Slamming the door and locking it, I jerked both of us to the ground.

"Speak," I said, freaking out.

"There's a Demon out there," Cher said, pointing to the door. With her left hand clutching the blowtorch, she reached into her pocket with her right and retrieved her lip liner. She proceeded to go to town. By the time she was done, she looked like Bozo the Clown holding a blowtorch.

My stomach dropped to my toes and my eyes narrowed. "Demon?" How in the hell did my overly made-up agent know about Demons? She was human. "Have you been drinking?"

"Do I look drunk to you?" she demanded.

"Umm… kind of," I said with an apologetic wince.

"Fair enough," she agreed. "I've had a couple hard ciders and a Valium, but I'm not drunk. I drove over and didn't get pulled over once."

"Congrats," I said. "And there's no such thing as Demons."

Cher rolled her eyes. "LA is filled with vipers and Demons. Trust me on that."

"Vipers?" I asked, worried there was some other fucking species that I wasn't aware of.

"Hell to the yes," Cher said, pulling a can of hard cider out of her Prada bag and popping the top. "I came over all excited to tell you that you've been booked on all the nighttime talk shows and I saw her."

"Saw who?"

"The fifty-five-year-old whore who banged my fourth husband before I took him to the cleaners for all he was worth," Cher said, chugging her cider. "Dina Slimeyass-bitchface."

"That's a real name?" I asked, not following at all.

"Hell yes, it is. Saw her walking her damned poodles. Hooker's had so much work done, her face looks like a rubber mask. Almost firebombed the bitch. I actually liked Herb. Damn shame he couldn't keep his pecker in his pants."

I almost puked with relief. Cher hadn't been talking about a real supernatural event. "Wait," I said, making sure I had it right. "You mean a woman, not an actual Demon?"

Cher stared at me like I'd gone and lost it. She would not be wrong. "Not a real Demon, but if there was a real Demon, Dina Slimeyassbitchface would fit the bill," she said, reaching into her bag and pulling out another hard cider. "Drink this. You look like you need it more than I do."

Crap. I needed to get Cher out of here. The chance of Nip Slip and Ophelia the mega-bitch coming back soon was high. I might be tempted to electrocute Ophelia again, and I didn't want Cher in the middle of a magical shitshow. However, if she left, there was a good possibility she would use one of my multiple blowtorches on Dina Slimeyassbitchface. That could land my agent in jail. I didn't need that. If I lived, we had a TV show to do. Even if I didn't, there was still a TV show to do.

"Cher," I said, trying to gauge how wasted she was. Her eyes were not right. There was no way she was driving anywhere. However, I knew of a fabulous babysitter. "Sean wants you to pop over and read the new script. It's perfect that you stopped by! You want to go now?"

Cher sucked back the cider intended for me then belched. "Sure do! Your brother is one hell of a sitcom writer!"

"Great," I said, grabbing my phone and texting Sean that Cher was coming over, and that I needed Cher, Man-mom and him to stay in their house until I gave the all clear. "Let's just walk you on over and—"

And that's when one of my bodyguards poofed back into my living room, screaming like the world was about to blow up. Nip Slip had paled to the point she looked like she was about to pass out. "It's her," she hissed. "We have to kill her."

Cher was flabbergasted but tried to go with the flow. "Where in the hell did she come from?"

"Back door," I lied with a wince.

Cher nodded and fired up the blowtorch. "I got it! We talking about Dina Slimeyassbitchface?"

"Who?" Rhoda asked, confused.

"Yes," I chimed in, opening up the front door and pushing Cher out of it. "She's next door at Sean's. Haul ass over there."

I blanched when I saw Ophelia outside on my front walkway. She was missing an arm and a leg, and was bleeding profusely. "Help me," she begged.

"What the FUCK?" Cher bellowed. "Did Dina Slimeyassbitchface do this to you?"

"Help me," Ophelia choked out. "She lies."

"Oh, I know she lies," Cher said, pulling a pair of night-vision goggles out of her purse and putting them on. "Dina Slimeyassbitchface is a lying sack of shit. I will avenge you, bleeding lady. Do not worry!"

"Oh my God," I muttered, freaking out. "This is not happening."

"End her. End Ophelia," Nip Slip snarled from behind me. "She's the one who betrayed you, Cecily Bloom. Kill her now. Scum like her does not deserve to live."

"Wait," Cher said, wildly confused. "So, Dina Slimeyassbitchface isn't who we're after?"

Something felt way the heck off here. I backed away from both Nip Slip and the bloody Ophelia. Grabbing the blowtorch from Cher, I situated myself on my front lawn where I could see both of my Demonic bodyguards. Sadly, Cher was going to need more therapy than normal. Getting her out of here wasn't an option.

"Stay behind me," I ordered, shoving the tiny woman out of harm's way then letting my gaze bounce between the two Demons who were supposed to be protecting me. "Explain what's going on."

"She invited Demons in," Rhoda hissed, pointing at the barely alive Ophelia.

"No," Ophelia choked out.

"Yes," Rhoda shouted. "She opened the ward right up and invited them in. I stopped her. I saved you. I'm a hero!"

"Interesting," I said, feeling my anger well up.

I didn't need a blowtorch. I *was* a damned blowtorch. "So, you're saying Ophelia invited flaming assholes inside the warded area?"

"Yes," Rhoda insisted.

"And they came in?" I inquired, holding back my fury with effort.

"They did," Rhoda assured me. "Came right in. I killed all of them then had to fight off Ophelia. She did her best to feed me to the animals."

"No. No," Ophelia whispered. "No."

"Yes," Rhoda said. "End her, Cecily Bloom. It's your right."

I nodded and walked over to Ophelia. Keeping my back to Nip Slip, I squatted down and stared at the blonde bitch. "I believe you," I whispered. My Demon Goddess mother had warded the area. From what Abaddon had told me, no one but him was allowed to choose which Demons were permitted inside—not Rhoda, and certainly not Ophelia.

No bad Demons had gotten inside the ward… No. That was

incorrect. Rhoda Spark was a very bad Demon and a brilliant actress. She was also about to go down. Now to figure out what to do with her…

"MOTHERFUCKER," Cher bellowed as she dove for a blowtorch and fired it up. "That's my producer. Nobody messes with my business!"

My chest tightened to the point of pain as I watched Rhoda drag the defenseless Abaddon to the front porch by his hair. His furious grunt of pain as she pressed a dagger into his neck filled me with rage.

The purple fire sword burst from my hand. "Let him go before I take your head off."

I gasped as she slit his throat and thick blood oozed from the wound, so he couldn't speak. His gaze was focused on me as he clutched his neck.

This was my fault. He'd taken my pain from the spell the Grim Reaper had cast to help me control my power, and now he couldn't defend himself against one of his crazed underlings. The traitorous Demon laughed as she held him tightly to her body. Her unhinged cackle would stay with me for an eternity.

"You want your Demon?" Nip Slip reveled in the power she held over Abaddon in his weakened state. "He'll live for now, but only if you stay back. If you don't, I'll make sure his soul never sees the light of this realm again."

"Move away from him and you might live," I ground out.

She rolled her eyes. "You're playing out of your league, Baby Demon. If you want him, you'll have to come after him. He'll be hanging out with Pandora until then."

I felt as if my heart was being ripped from my chest. "I'll find you, and I'll make you pay for this."

"See ya," she snarled. "Wouldn't wanna be ya, Cecily Bloom."

And on that horrifying note, Rhoda vanished with the Demon I was falling in love with.

"Jesus Christ!" Cher shouted, kicking off her heels and sprinting over to Ophelia. "Hang on, Demon. I've got you."

I squinted at my agent, certain I'd just heard her wrong. "What did you call Ophelia?"

Cher rolled her eyes and removed her hot-pink jacket and her ivory silk blouse. "Gave this shit up centuries ago. Can't fucking believe I'm jumping back in."

"What?" I asked as the batshit crazy woman removed her bra. She was now silicone tits to the wind.

"Is the bloody one a bad gal or a good gal?"

"Good, mostly," I said. "Are you stripping?"

"Don't I wish," Cher grumbled as shimmering white wings burst from her back. "Gonna heal the Demon. And it might have been nice for you to have clued me in that *you're* a dang Demon, Cecily."

My mouth fell open. "What are you?" I whispered as my half-naked agent squatted down and gently touched Ophelia.

"Used to be a fucking Angel," Cher griped. "Gave it up but apparently, once an Angel, always an Angel."

"You can heal Ophelia?" I asked as Sean, Man-mom and Uncle Joe came barreling out of Sean's house.

"Yessssss," Cher hissed. "Means I'm gonna have to be a working Angel again for a century, but whatever. Worse things could happen."

"Speechless." I watched the golden light emanating from Cher surround Ophelia. The Demon slowly healed before our eyes.

Ophelia gingerly sat up and tested her new limbs. "Where's Abaddon?" she demanded as she glanced around in panic.

"Nip Slip took him," I told her. "Said he'd be with Pandora. Does that mean they went into the Darkness?" Fear gripped me tightly. Abaddon, with his power on the fritz, was a sitting duck.

"No," Ophelia said with a shudder. "They went somewhere far worse than the Darkness."

Her ominous reply increased my anxiety. "What's worse than the Darkness?"

The blonde Demon shook her head and let out a slow breath. "Vegas."

"As in Las Vegas?" I asked. "In Nevada?"

"Yes," she replied, still looking horrified. "Sin City is a favorite of the Underworld—especially Pandora."

"Huh," I muttered. Could shit get any more bizarre?

Cher, who was having a near religious experience at the mention of the city where dreams go to die, quipped, "Guess we're going to Vegas this weekend!" She put her bra back on and took a chug from another hard cider she pulled out of her bag.

"Thank you for healing me, Angel," Ophelia said, bowing her head to Cher. "I owe you."

"Damn right you do, Demon," she muttered. Then she turned to my brother. "Sean, you have a script for me? I can read it on the drive to Vegas. I'm damned good at multitasking."

Sean, who looked dumbstruck, or maybe he was just seriously stoned, nodded his head and handed her the script.

"We're driving? Not poofing?" I asked.

"Driving," Ophelia confirmed. "A poof would announce our arrival. We don't want that."

"Got it. And just a heads up," I said. "Nip Slip dies."

"I'm down with that," Ophelia said.

"Works for me," Cher agreed.

My father, who'd been quiet up until that point, asked, "Can I make a suggestion?"

"By all means," I said, walking into my house and grabbing my car keys as my dad followed.

He retrieved a card from his pocket. It was black with a number embossed on the front in shimmering silver foil—it almost looked alive. He handed it to me. "Call this cellphone number," he said.

I cocked my head at Man-mom. "Why? Who does it belong to?"

"Your mother," he said. "I think it's time you met her."

I stared at the card. Under normal circumstances, I'd have flushed the card down the toilet.

The circumstances were not normal.

I didn't have to like the woman who'd given birth to me then left. I didn't have to respect her. However, I was in a seriously shitty position. If it was just me I was concerned about, I wouldn't call her.

It wasn't just me.

It was Abaddon, and I wasn't willing to lose him.

I understood the game. Pandora had stolen something I wanted. She planned to destroy me when I showed up to get Abaddon back.

That was the game.

I just didn't know the rules… yet.

However, I played to win. Always. I wasn't about to change my ways now.

Glancing down at the card again, I realized my hand trembled. Whatever. I didn't need my mother's love or approval.

That ship had sailed forty years ago. I only needed her skill and expertise.

She owed me that.

She owed Abaddon that.

I dialed the number and held my breath.

As the Underworld turned upside down, so did the days of my life.

CHAPTER TWO

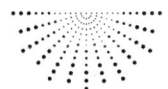

"Who did you call back at the house, Cecily?" Cher asked groggily, waking up in the backseat of Judy, my pickup truck.

We'd been driving for an hour. Most of it had been silent since Cher had been sleeping. Well, silent other than her snoring. Ophelia and I didn't have much in common. We'd avoided conversation. That worked just fine for me.

As to Cher's question, I wasn't sure how much to share about the phone call to my mother. It wasn't clear what the blonde bimbo Demon knew. Was she aware I was Lilith's daughter? Granted, Ophelia wasn't as evil as Rhoda, but that didn't mean she was good… or trustworthy. The less confessing the better, at this point.

"Friend of my dad's," I replied. "Someone who he thought could help."

Ophelia sat in the front passenger seat and rolled her eyes. "I thought your dad was human."

"Don't think," I said. "It doesn't seem to go well for you."

Cher cackled. Ophelia flipped me off. I didn't care. I'd successfully diverted the conversation. Plus, my mother didn't even answer the call. I'd left a freaking message with all the particulars. The sound of her voice had thrown me for a hot sec, but I'd soldiered on. Strangely, it had been familiar. I couldn't place it, but it had resonated. I didn't have time to dissect my crazy. If I survived the weekend, I'd do that in therapy next week minus all the otherworldly crap.

"Anyone thirsty?" Cher inquired.

"Do you have anything non-alcoholic?" I asked, knowing it was probably a long shot.

"Lemme look," she said, digging into her bag. "Nope."

"I'm good," I said, shaking my head.

"Do you have whiskey?" Ophelia asked. "The good stuff?"

"No can do, but I've got a hard lemonade," Cher answered.

"Fine," Ophelia said in a snotty tone. "I suppose that will do."

I wasn't delighted with her tone or the fact that there were open liquor bottles in the car. Whatever. As long as I wasn't drinking, we'd live.

Or would we?

"Tits Magee," I said, glancing over at Ophelia as she downed the lemonade in one noisy and unladylike gulp.

"You talking to me, over-the-hill former child star?" she questioned with a raised brow and a burp.

"Point to both of you," Cher announced from the back with a chuckle. "That means it's one to one."

"Well, played," I told the Demon. "How old are you again?"

"Five hundred, bitch," she reminded me.

"Just checking," I said with a grin. "Not sure your over-the-hill comment holds water, girlfriend."

"Touché," she replied. "How old is the Angel?"

It was a really good question. I was still absorbing the fact that Cher was an Angel and not just my beloved agent who wore too much lipliner and power suits that were two sizes too small.

"Rude," Cher grumbled. "No comment."

"Seriously?" I asked with a laugh.

"Seriously," she replied. "Too much to handle and even saying the number aloud will give me gas. Since we're trapped in the car together for another three hours, no one wants me to get the toots."

I was insanely curious, but I'd been downwind of my agent when she'd been gassy in the past. It wasn't a place I wanted to go ever again.

"Will you tell me someday?" I asked.

"When you win an Emmy, yes," she shot back.

The chances of that were slim, but not out of the realm of possibility. Of course, I'd have to live long enough to shoot the show to even be considered.

Speaking of living... "Ophelia," I began.

"That's my name, don't wear it out."

I groaned. For being five hundred, she had the maturity level of an elementary school kid.

"Shall I go back to Tits Magee?" I inquired.

"Sure, Seymour Asscrack," she countered.

I laughed. Cher choked on her cider. I was glad she was Immortal. I didn't know the Heimlich Maneuver.

"Nice one, Stella Virgin," I said.

This time Ophelia laughed. Cher was still choking.

"Cher, you okay?"

"Yep. Some spit just went down the wrong damn pipe hole," she said, still coughing but giving me a thumbs up. "Keep going."

The Demon rubbed her hands together and grinned. "Well, Ura Snotball, it's interesting to see you've got game."

"Oh, I've got plenty of game, Maya Buttreeks," I informed her.

Thankfully, a few years back, Sean and I had created a list of the most disgusting names possible after a few *special* gummies. I was armed and ready. Yes, I'd reverted to middle school, but laughing in the potential face of death was kind of relaxing.

"Let's go, Hairy Poppins," she challenged. "Winner gets a million bucks."

"Oh my God," I said with a laugh. "I don't have a million lying around, Dill Doe. Pick another prize."

Ophelia shrugged. "The winner gets a full spa day at the Four Seasons, Gazzy Colon. Compliments of the loser."

"Works for me, Jenny Taylia."

"Dyin' back here," Cher shouted with a belly laugh. "And I want in, Lee Keyrear and Mike Rotchburns."

"This will not end well," I stated with a grin.

"Nothing *ends* well, Vye Agra," Ophelia pointed out. "The key is to leave before it's over."

"Not my style, Sheeza Freak," I told her. "I'm a see-it-to-the-end kind of gal."

Ophelia eyed me with pity. "That equates to dead, Yuri Nator."

While the information being shot back and forth was very serious, the game was still being played. Fine. I could do that.

I shrugged. "So, Lou Briccant, is there a chance that we're being chased by flaming Demon assholes at the moment?"

Ophelia glanced out of the passenger side window. "There's always a chance that death is around the corner, Mary Juana. The fun is to stay one step ahead."

Our ideas of fun were vastly different. My stomach clenched and I gripped the steering wheel so tightly my knuckles turned white. There was a good chance that both Ophelia and Rhoda were in cahoots with Pandora. I might be driving right into my demise. However, I wasn't turning back. Pandora had Abaddon, and I wasn't about to leave him in her clutches.

"Hang on, Max E. Pad," Cher yelled from the backseat. "You owe me for saving your ass. If we're in danger right now, speak up. You do not want me to punch you in the back of your head. Cause if I do, my fist will end up in your mouth."

Ophelia had the smarts to look alarmed. I was slightly alarmed too. I'd had Judy detailed last week. Blood spatters and flying brain matter would suck. However, dying would suck worse.

"Tell me why I should trust you," I ground out, turning the wheel sharply and pulling over onto the shoulder of the highway.

The Demon looked bored. "You shouldn't."

Inhaling deeply and turning the ignition off, I went over my options. All of them were bad. If I put her out of the car, I didn't know where I was going once we hit Vegas. However, if she ended me before we got there, that was on me.

"Who are you loyal to?" I demanded.

My body heated up quickly and it felt like a mini-inferno was bubbling underneath my skin. I hoped to hell and back that old Uncle Gideon the Grim Reaper had indeed helped me control the enchanted shitshow I'd been blessed with. Lighting myself on fire right now would be incredibly counterproductive.

The cab of my truck filled with so much magic, I quickly rolled down the windows. I didn't need to suffocate myself with my own power.

Ophelia appeared shocked. Cher clapped like I'd just won an Oscar.

"Answer me," I snapped.

"The Goddess Lilith," she said, pressing herself against the passenger-side door.

"Prove it," I told her.

I had no clue how she could prove it. I didn't know how I would prove it, if asked. Hell, I didn't know if I was even loyal to Lilith. However, my mother did seem to be the lesser of two evils at this point.

The Demon looked bewildered. "I can't."

"I've got this," Cher grunted, climbing over the seat and getting in Ophelia's face. She stuck her thumbs into the Demon's ears then headbutted her. Shit, that had to smart.

The sound of noggin on noggin was awful. I thought that Ophelia had been rendered unconscious, but thankfully she was just dazed. Cher was out of her mind.

"Umm… what are you doing?" I whispered, horrified.

"I'm in her head. I can tell if she's lying. Hurts like a mofo, so go quick. Ask her whatever you need to know. Last time I did this was thousands of years ago and I ended up with a killer hemorrhoid—lots of pressure."

All of a sudden, we seemed to be lost in the plot of a really crappy B horror/sci-fi movie. I was worried about the Demon. She was seriously pale. Although, I reminded myself that Cher had healed Ophelia after she'd lost an arm and a leg. I was pretty sure my insane agent could heal a concussion too. I hoped she didn't have to remove her bra to do it.

"Not joshin' ya, Cecily," Cher said. "I can feel my butt burning."

"Got it," I said with the inappropriate urge to laugh. "Who are you loyal to? Lilith or Pandora?"

"Lilith," Ophelia answered in a monotone.

"Truth," Cher said, panting hard.

"Where are we going in Vegas?" I asked, just in case she bailed on us.

"Near Old Vegas—a casino about three miles south. Immortals like the area. Humans don't go there. Too seedy," she answered in the same dead tone.

"Truth," Cher supplied.

"Name of the casino," I pressed, racking my brain for questions.

"Golden Showers Bet and Bed," Ophelia said.

"Gotta be a lie," I muttered. Who in the hell would name a place of business Golden Showers?

"Truth," Cher wheezed.

I stood corrected. Taste was obviously relative.

"Are you going to try to kill me?" I asked.

"Not unless Lilith decrees it," Ophelia replied.

"Truth."

Cher didn't look great and neither did Ophelia. I needed to wrap it up. "Why does Pandora want Abaddon?"

"Because he doesn't want her," Ophelia said with a weak laugh. "She knows he wants you."

"She's telling the truth," Cher said.

"So, Pandora isn't after me for anything more *specific*?" I asked, wondering if I had the scenario all wrong. Was it pure jealousy? Did she not know who I was?

"Why would Pandora be after you? Do you know her? Did you beat the bitch out of a role?" Cher asked.

Again, I almost laughed. With Cher, everything was about show business. Instead, I shrugged and waited for Ophelia to answer.

"If you're the Demon Goddess who comes from two

worlds, who shall bring on the end, then yes. If not, no." Her voice was getting weaker and Cher was sweating like she was experiencing menopause for a hundred women.

"Shit," I said with a shudder. I wasn't sure if Pandora knew, but if the flaming assholes were any indication, then she did. However, it seemed as if Ophelia was blissfully unaware of my identity. Maybe. But then again, I'd thought Rhoda Spark aka Nip Slip wasn't that bad. My character judgement and lie detector skills weren't great lately. "Enough. Cher, stop. Let her go."

Ophelia slumped forward and gasped for air.

Cher gingerly touched her butt and winced. "Another damn hemorrhoid," she griped. "The things I do for my clients…"

This time I did laugh. The absurdity was too much. "I'm sorry," I told her.

"Nah," she said, climbing over the seat and into the back. "I got stock in butt cream. Best investment I ever made. Did you learn what you need to know?"

I nodded. "For now, yes."

Cher heaved a sigh of relief. "That's good. My ass couldn't take much more."

I looked back at the tiny dynamo of a woman and blew her a kiss. "I thank you and I thank your ass."

"We both say, you're welcome," Cher assured me with a chuckle as she popped the top on another hard cider.

Ophelia's breathing was still labored, but she didn't look like she was going to pass out anymore. "Do not *ever* do that again, Angel," she ground out, pressing her temples.

"Or?" Cher demanded from the backseat as her eyes turned a blinding gold.

The entire interior was bathed in golden light. For a hot sec, I worried that Ophelia and I might combust since we were

Demons. The rules of this ridiculous world I'd been recently thrust into were wildly unclear.

I glanced down to make sure I wasn't smoldering. Nope. So far, so good.

"Or you will be very sorry," Ophelia snapped.

"Doubtful," Cher replied. "I eat assholes like you for breakfast."

I gagged. "You're a cannibal?"

"Nah," she replied with a laugh. "Didn't mean it literally. Eating a Demon would constipate me. I like staying regular. Although, I do know a gal who ate some Angels a long time ago. Nasty business, but she's a nice broad aside from her toothpick habit. It was shortly after that I turned in my Angel Card. Bunch of crazy assholes."

"Right," I said, completely grossed out. I was unsure if she knew she'd get plugged up because she'd eaten a Demon in the past or if she was just spitballing. I decided it was in my digestive tract's best interest not to pursue the subject. And I never wanted to meet her toothpick-loving, Angel-eating buddy. "So, umm… are we good to keep going? Everyone happy?"

"Are you an idiot?" Ophelia hissed.

"Occasionally," I replied, starting the truck back up. I had to agree with the Demon. Asking everyone if they were happy was idiotic.

"Phone's ringing," Cher said, announcing the obvious.

I grabbed my cellphone, glanced at the incoming call and swallowed my gasp with effort.

My mother was calling me back.

I'd memorized the number then eaten the card. It was a move I'd done plenty of times on my infamous TV show *Camp Bite*, as a kid playing a vampire who solved supernatural crimes. Of course, since it was a TV show, I didn't really have to swallow the cards. On the rare occasion that I did have to swallow, they'd made me edible cards.

The card that Man-mom had given me was not edible. It was dry and tasted a little bit like paint—not surprising since my dad was a self-proclaimed multimedia artist. The fact that it had seemed alive was disturbing, but I was sure Lilith wouldn't want her cellphone number getting around… so I ate it.

Why I was protecting her from telemarketers was beyond me.

Quickly turning the ignition off again, I opened up the truck door. "I'll be right back."

My hands shook and my skin felt clammy. The marching band playing in my stomach had turned it up to eleven. I had five more rings before it went to voicemail. My entire life, I'd dreamed of talking to the woman who gave birth to me. Now that it was a reality, I was pretty sure I was about to puke.

"She's not calling because she cares," I mumbled as I walked away from the car. "She couldn't give a shit about me."

Inhaling deeply, I accepted the call. "Yes?" I ground out through clenched teeth.

"Hold for Lilith," a voice said.

I rolled my eyes. "You've got to be fucking kidding me," I muttered.

"I am," the voice said with a musical giggle. "It's me. Lilith. Hello, Cecily. What can I do for you?"

The question was so loaded, I was speechless for a moment. Hearing her say my name hurt. Her question was like a dagger in the heart. What could she do for me?

She could have loved me.

She could have stayed.

She could have visited me. I would have carried her secret to the grave.

The list was long.

The list was irrelevant.

"Did you get my message, Lilith?" I demanded, trying to hold on to my composure.

She was silent on the other end for a long moment. "Quite formal, Cecily."

"If you were hoping I'd call you mom, you're shit out of luck. Of course, I could call you egg donor if that's more to your liking." I pressed my lips together and sternly reminded myself why I'd called. This was not a mother-daughter reunion. I needed her help in getting Abaddon back safely. That was it. Period.

"Calling me Lilith will be fine. And yes, I received your message," she replied. "I've sent people to find and retrieve Abaddon. You must go back to LA."

"Not happening," I told her. "He got taken because of me. He's in a weakened state. I don't shirk my responsibilities—like others I know. Or rather… don't know."

Again, she was silent. I felt as low as a person could go. I wasn't ten. I was forty. The woman had never been part of my life and she wasn't going to be now. Letting go of my childhood fantasies would be a damn fine plan.

I was an actress. This was simply a role. A make-believe role. It just sucked that my heart was involved.

"I'm sorry," I whispered. "That was uncalled for."

"So you'll return to LA?"

"No. I'm going to Vegas. I apologized for the other part," I admitted.

"Anger is healthy unless it consumes you," Lilith said in a

curt and chilly tone. "It's unwise for you to be near Pandora. I forbid it."

I rolled my eyes. "You're not the boss of me, Lilith," I snapped. "I have a purple freaking fire sword and a whole lot of pent-up fury. I'll be just fine."

"You have no clue what you'll be dealing with," she snapped right back. "Go home, Cecily. Immediately. You're incapable of winning this fight. Go. Home."

I laughed. "You have no clue what I'm capable of," I said in an icy tone. "And you... can go to hell. Oh, wait... you're already there."

"Fine," she said, furious. "I will see you in Vegas."

"Don't bet on it," I said rudely then hung up on her.

I stood frozen to the spot. What the hell had I just done? My goal was saving Abaddon. Although, she did say she was sending people...

"Motherfucker," I yelled into the starless, inky black night. "How much of an idiot can I be?"

The sound echoed eerily in the quiet and I almost hurled my phone into the darkness. Gripping it tightly so my body didn't disobey my brain, I stomped my foot like a toddler. I'd already done enough stupid stuff. Losing my phone would be beyond.

"Do you want me to answer that?" Ophelia called out from the car.

I turned and glared. "If you want to live, then no," I shouted back at her.

She wasn't as dumb as I thought. The Demon didn't say a word.

Shaking off my fury so I didn't set myself aflame, I marched back over to the truck, got in and started it. It had been a shitty day that had morphed into a shittier night. I was driving into something that was probably way over my head, but I wasn't going back to LA. I wasn't a quitter. I never had been and today didn't seem like a good day to start. I'd always thought being an actress was my happily ever after. I was beginning to suspect that Abaddon might hold that title.

Even if he didn't, I wasn't going to desert him. He'd saved me multiple times in the short amount of time I'd known him.

I was going to repay the favor… even if it killed me.

CHAPTER THREE

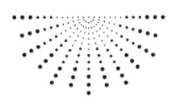

"Love me some Vegas," Cher announced, oohing and ahhing over the lights on the main Strip. "Too bad Demons don't like the Bellagio. I won half a mil there a few years back."

"You did?" I asked, shocked.

I'd never won crap in Vegas. My poker face was piss-poor, according to Sean and Man-mom. Plus, I didn't love crowds. I hadn't been to Vegas in years. Used to come a lot back when I was married for a brief and crappy stint to the idiot rock star, Slash Gordon. Back in the day, the hair-band asshole was a big deal. Today, he'd be lucky to be an opening act.

I'd gotten married in Vegas, and caught my soon-to-be ex-husband in an orgy with groupies in Vegas. The memories here were not great. And I was under no illusion that I would be making terrific memories in the next twenty-four to forty-eight hours.

"Yep!" Cher confirmed. "Won a cool million at the Venetian a decade ago too."

Ophelia whipped around and squinted at Cher. "Did you cheat?"

Cher gasped and wagged her finger at the Demon.

"Did you?" Ophelia demanded.

Cher took her time answering. Now, I was interested.

"No comment," Cher mumbled.

"Oh my God," I said with a half laugh, half groan. "You're an Angel. Angels aren't supposed to cheat. Seems more like a Demon kind of thing to do."

"You got that right," Ophelia said, putting her hand up for a high-five.

I didn't leave her hanging even though I wasn't exactly stoked to be on the Demon side of my last statement.

"Angels are assholes," Cher said. "Bunch of golden-eyed, white-wing-sporting pricks."

"Demons aren't much better," Ophelia chimed in.

As I didn't have anything to add, I was quiet as I navigated the Strip in my pickup. Hitting someone would be bad. It was after midnight and the crowds milling around had definitely consumed their fair share of alcohol.

"I really don't like this city," I said, taking in all the pawn shops in between the casinos. "Makes me kind of sad."

"It's an illusion," Ophelia said. "All of it—the sparkling lights, the free booze, the shows with beautiful women… it hides a rancid underbelly of addiction and desperation."

I glanced over at her in surprise. Ophelia was deeper than her appearance led one to believe.

"Is that why Demons like it here?" I asked, checking the map on my phone. We were about fifteen minutes away from our destination.

She shook her head and stared unseeingly out of the window. "Not all Demons love it. I don't."

I wanted her to keep talking. Anything I could learn would be helpful… or at least it would be something.

"Why?" I pressed.

She shrugged. "Those loyal to the Goddess Lilith don't come here."

"Why?" I asked again.

"You're annoying," Ophelia said.

"Correct. Why don't Demons who are loyal to Lilith come here?"

The Demon in my car—other than me—sighed dramatically. "One, because it's Pandora's territory. Two, while Demons can't morally harm humans, some quite enjoy siphoning the desperate and depraved energy this shithole gives off."

"Like a Succubus?" I asked, recalling tales from mythology that I'd loved in my youth.

"Sure," she answered. "Except they don't kill or eat their prey."

Swallowing back my bile, I just nodded. Thankfully, Succubi weren't real.

"Those whackjobs are nuts," Cher commented from the back, relining her already lined lips.

"Wait. What?" I asked with a wince. "They exist?"

"Darn tootin'," she replied. "Good-lookin' sons of bitches, but right out of their damn minds."

"No such thing as a real Succubus," Ophelia said.

"Wrong," Cher countered. "I've learned a crapload in my twelve million years."

I gasped. I wasn't sure if it was because Succubi were living among us or because Cher was twelve freaking million years old.

"Whoopsidoodle," Cher said with a laugh. "Cat's out of the bag."

"Twelve million?" I asked. "For real?"

"As a heart attack," she replied with a sigh. "Immortality, while nice in theory, is a bitch in real life."

"Word," Ophelia agreed.

"Getting depressed here," I said, shaking my head. "Am I Immortal?"

Ophelia shrugged. "Don't know. Is your dad your real dad? Biologically?"

"He is," I replied.

"So, it's your mother that's a Demon?" she continued.

"Correct." It was now clear that Ophelia didn't know I was Lilith's daughter. That was a relief.

"Up for grabs then," Cher told me. "Not many hybrids I know of."

"You know people like me?" I asked, surprised.

Cher powdered her overly made-up face and scrunched her nose. "Actually, nope."

Ophelia reached back and pilfered another hard lemonade from Cher's bag. "You're half Demon, half human. Chances are you'll just live longer than a regular human lifespan but not forever. Doubtful that you're Immortal. Congrats."

Crap. I wasn't so sure I was half human. From what Abaddon had said, it didn't look like I was falling into the hybrid category anymore. I had two Goat Eyes instead of one and could most likely blow up the continental U.S. if I wasn't careful. I had no clue how I felt about living forever and now wasn't the time to figure it out.

"Hold on," I said. "*If* I'm Immortal, I can't die. Right?"

"Wrong," Cher told me.

"What she said," Ophelia added, downing her drink then gracing us with a burp that should have belonged to a man three times her size. "If, and I stress the word *if*, you're Immortal, you're just harder to kill."

"Got it," I said. "Should we go straight to the casino?"

"Do we have a plan?" Ophelia asked.

"Umm… nope," I replied. It was a very good question.

"Then I'm gonna go with a big no on that," she said. "No plan means sure death. As much as living forever can suck, I'm not ready to bite it yet. I have a soap audition next week."

I bit my tongue. Pointing out she'd recently gotten fired from the soap *The Ocean is Deeply Moving* would be mean. She'd been heinous to me at the final callback, but in the end, she'd helped me dodge a career-destroying bullet.

"I've got a plan," Cher announced.

That scared me a lot. Cher's plans usually involved alcohol, Vicodin and lip liner.

"Let's hear it, Angel," Ophelia said.

"Hang on a sec," Cher said, scrolling on her phone.

I pulled into a strip mall and parked at the edge of the mostly empty lot. There was a hotel across the street missing the letters T and L. It said Hoe. Nice.

"Almost there," Cher muttered. "Cecily, do you remember when you almost landed that kids' show, *Lou's News*?"

I winced. The amount of embarrassing auditions I had in my trunk was mortifying. *Lou's News* was one of many. Although, it was one of the worst. "Wrong name of the show, but yes. Why do you know about that? You weren't my agent back then."

"Tape made the rounds with the casting directors and landed in my lap," she informed me.

I screamed. There was nothing else I could do other than blow up my pickup truck. I loved Judy. Setting her on fire was not happening. "You're kidding me," I choked out.

"What happened?" Ophelia asked gleefully.

"Nothing," I snapped. "And Cher, why did you bring that up?"

"It's all about believing you can do it," Cher explained. "You showed the can-do attitude we need right now! You believed you could fly and knocked out two of your teeth on camera proving it. You got right back up and did it again, causing you to split your forehead open and need forty-two stitches. You were a twenty-year-old genius. I've never seen such commitment in all my years in the biz. It was that video that convinced me to become an agent. I went after you like you were a dog who had my bone. You might not have landed the role, but you gave my life purpose, Cecily Bloom. If you thought you could fly, I knew I could become an agent with absolutely no knowledge of show business. It's worked out real good!"

I screamed again. It was far better than electrocuting my agent. She'd just taken on a new hemorrhoid for me. "That is the worst story I've ever heard.

"*Please* tell me you have the video on your phone," Ophelia begged.

"Just the part where Cecily knocks her teeth out," Cher said, still searching. "Got the whole thing on my desktop computer at the office. Fucking brilliant."

It was *not* fucking brilliant. It was fucking horrifying. All the memories came flooding back. I hadn't wanted to be on another kids' show after my years on *Camp Bite*, but the pickings had been slim.

I closed my eyes and leaned back in my seat. If Cher found it, I didn't need to see it. I'd lived it.

The waiting room was bright green. I'd dressed in colorful sweats because I'd been told the final callback would be athletic. Since I didn't own colorful sweats, I'd made a quick run to the mall. Looking ridiculous was clearly part of the plan. Six times I'd tried to get out of the final callback, but no go. My gut told me that I should bail. While my excuses had been pathetic, I hadn't grown big enough actress balls to stand up for myself yet.

I'd rolled my eyes hard when my agent at the time had informed me of the colorful sweats requirement... and that she'd drop me as a client if I bagged on the final round. I'd already "jumped funny" for the casting people and producers for over an hour in front of a green screen just the week before. Pulling muscles I didn't know I had was awful. I'd had to get a massage after that hot mess.

Yet, here I was... at the final callback. I'd almost stayed back in the waiting room, but I was not a quitter.

About ten network execs and three casting people sat in chairs drinking coffee and looking rabidly excited. It made my stomach hurt. I waved. They waved back. My competition, who I'd named Obnoxious Girl with Dumbass Pigtails, did a somersault, landed at their feet and saluted them. They laughed with delight.

Shit. Why didn't I think of that? Maybe because it was stupid? I was very aware that Obnoxious Girl with Dumbass Pigtails wasn't a very nice name for me to have secretly given her, but she'd not so secretly been calling me Vampire Girl throughout the seven callbacks we'd been through together. I suppose she thought that would psyche me out. She was wrong. I'd developed seriously thick skin during the years I'd logged in the biz. Being the Vampire Girl had bought me a house and a car. Obnoxious Girl with Dumbass Pigtails could kiss my ass.

The wrinkle was that there was a third person in the running who I'd never seen. He was a quiet guy with a friendly smile.

"Hey there! Hi there! Ho there, kids!" the director shouted at Obnoxious Girl with Dumbass Pigtails, Quiet Guy and me as he entered the audition space.

"Hey there! Hi there! Ho there to you too!" my competition shouted in her outdoor voice.

Dammit. Her sweats were more colorful than mine. My need to win fired up inside me. The fact that the job would put me into traction didn't matter.

"Hey doodley do there! Hi woodley woo there! Ho—not the bad kind—there to you too!" I screamed at the top of my lungs.

I wanted to die, but the attention was on me now. Winning. Although, everyone looked confused. I realized I probably shouldn't have made reference to a hooker since this was a children's program.

"Hi everyone," Quiet Guy said politely.

The producers nodded, seemingly impressed that he could speak at a socially acceptable volume. I made a mental note to tone it down.

"Okay kiddos," the director who called himself Papa announced. "We want to see if you can fly!"

I squinted at him. Papa was missing a few screws if he thought anyone could actually fly. "Literally?"

"You betcha," he shouted with a spastic thumbs up.

"Awesome!" Obnoxious Girl with Dumbass Pigtails yelled, doing an aerial cartwheel.

The crowd went nuts. I was no longer winning.

There was no way I could do an aerial without breaking my neck. However, I was thirty to forty percent sure I could do a diving front roll. The odds weren't the best, but if I did the dive in front of the camera filming us, it would look like I was flying.

"Who wants to go next?" Papa shouted.

"I will," Quiet Guy said with a shy smile.

"Have at it," Papa screamed, jumping up and down.

Papa was alarming. I hoped he wasn't the main director of the show. The urge to throat punch him was strong.

Quiet Guy walked to the center of the room and put his arms out in front of him. He slowly rocked back and forth as he appeared to be *looking down at the world from the sky.* "Such a lovely place," he said with an adorable grin. "The colors make my heart sing. And look! I can see my house. I feel like I'm a big airplane. It's amazing! Would you like to fly with me?" he asked the camera. "Great! Let's fly together."

I tried to gauge which flying the producers liked better. It was difficult to tell. They clapped just as loudly for Quiet Guy as they did for Obnoxious Girl with Dumbass Pigtails. Personally, I liked Quiet Guy's gentle style, but decided to go with the dive roll.

It was a mistake. A huge mistake. One of the hugest mistakes I'd ever made.

"You ready for your turn, Cecily?" Papa asked, bouncing up and down.

It was scary watching a bald dude in his sixties called Papa bounce like a ball.

"I am," I said at a volume that was about halfway between Quiet Guy and Obnoxious Girl with Dumbass Pigtails. "Everyone, stand back. I'm about to fly!"

Obnoxious Girl with Dumbass Pigtails glared at me. Quiet Guy gave me an encouraging thumbs up and a sweet smile. The producers were on the edge of their seats. My confidence soared.

Taking a running start, I dove as I passed the camera. The cheers were music to my ears. As I went for the forward roll, it didn't quite go as planned. Instead of a roll, I face planted. Hard.

"I'm fine," I shouted, swiping away the sweat from my face that I didn't realize was blood. I was pretty sure I heard screams, but my ears were ringing. I ignored them. "Let me try that again!"

I wasn't certain, but I thought I heard Papa yell, NO. The ear ringing was loud. I spit out the hard gum in my mouth that I'd forgotten I was chewing and went back to my starting point. The producers were on their feet. I took that as a great sign.

It wasn't.

As I ran toward the camera, I realized that the gum I'd spit out were my teeth. Needless to say, that threw me for a loop. But I kept going. The show must always go on, even if you're bleeding and toothless. I misjudged the camera—probably due to the blood from my mouth that had spread to my eyes—and hit it as I dove. The sharp edge caught my forehead and it felt like I'd been slashed with a knife.

However, this time I did finish with a very nice forward roll.

Then I passed out. The last thing I recalled before I was out like a light, was Papa crying. Maybe he wasn't all that bad.

After a trip to the emergency room for stitches, I spent the next few weeks visiting the oral surgeon to get my teeth fixed. I was thrilled to learn Quiet Guy had nabbed the role. After all I'd been through, it would have chapped my butt to hear that Obnoxious Girl with Dumbass Pigtails had booked it.

I also fired my agent. All's well that ends well is mostly a bullshit statement, but this time it fit.

"Oh my God," Ophelia said with reverence, still staring at Cher's phone. "That was amazing."

I winced. Apparently while reliving my worst day ever in my head, they were watching it in full color.

"Screw you," I snapped. "You're not funny."

The Demon flipped me off. "Not trying to be, asshole. If I could do that I wouldn't be stuck on soaps or playing dead corpses wearing see-through lingerie on cop shows."

I squinted at her and tried to figure out if she was being genuine. If she was playing me, I'd electrocute her. "I played a corpse once," I admitted.

Her eyes grew huge. "Really?"

"Once," I told her. "And then I fired my agent."

"Wasn't me," Cher volunteered. "I'd never send you on something to be naked and dead."

"Well," Ophelia huffed. "I can't fly like you can, bitch. If I had your talent, I wouldn't have to take my clothes off to get paid."

I felt awful. What I'd just said was mean and unnecessary. "I'm sorry."

The Demon didn't respond.

Cher squinted at Ophelia for a long moment. "Who reps you?"

"Talent-Is-Us," Ophelia replied morosely.

"Can you act at all?" she asked the Demon.

Ophelia rested her head on the dashboard. "I don't know—probably not. I just figured I'd try it because LA is filled with Demons and jerks. Totally my comfort zone. I also have big tits."

I ignored the tits part. "Demons?" I asked. "Like real Demons?"

"Tons," Cher confirmed.

That was news to me.

"What's your dream role, Ophelia?" I asked.

She gave me a side glance. "You'll laugh."

"I won't," I promised, hoping to hell and back that she wasn't going to say the Meryl Streep role in a remake of *Sophie's Choice*.

"I want to be the next Vanna White," she blurted out.

"Brilliant," Cher shouted, dialing a number on her phone then handing it to Ophelia.

"Who am I calling?" she asked, confused.

"You're gonna leave a message. It's after hours," Cher explained. "Fire your agents. You have a new rep."

"You?" Ophelia whispered, sounding like a child on Christmas morning.

"Hell to the yes, girlfriend," Cher informed her. "I can get you a sub gig on the *Wheel of Fortune*. When Vanna retires, you'll have that job! I take fifteen percent and I'll negotiate like a bulldog. I do *not* fuck around when it comes to money."

Ophelia screamed. I joined her. Cher handed out hard ciders. Everyone indulged.

"Done," Ophelia shrieked as she handed Cher back her phone. "Would it be bad if Vanna suddenly moved to Tahiti?"

"Yes," I snapped. "You can't do anything to Vanna."

Cher walloped Ophelia in the back of her head. "You're gonna play by my rules now, Demon. We do not maim, relocate or, God forbid, kill anyone for a job. Am I clear?"

"Yes," she said. "Very clear. I agree completely. I was just checking."

I shook my head and groaned. We needed to get moving. "Okay. Back to the plan."

"You gals ready?" Cher asked, slipping out of her pink power jacket and rubbing her little hands together.

"No. But tell us." I held my breath and waited.

She told us.

Oh. My. God. My agent was insane.

CHAPTER FOUR

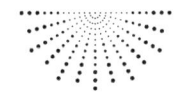

"No. No way. No how," I said, completely frustrated.

"It's brilliant," Cher insisted for the umpteenth time.

I could tell Ophelia was leaning towards going with the plan.

I was not.

"I don't sing. I don't dance, and there is no way I'm going to strip," I informed the crazy Angel.

Cher believed we could waltz right on into the casino and have full access to the place if we had an act. She also apparently had a hearing problem. "Picture this," she said, ignoring me and bouncing up and down on the bench seat of my truck. "We call you the Double D's! Get it? Demon and Demon. Two Demons!"

"Also, I have a fabulous set of double D's," Ophelia reminded us, lifting her shirt and displaying the goods. "I paid very good money for them."

I closed my eyes and sucked my bottom lip into my mouth. This was a terrible plan.

We didn't know where in the casino Abaddon was being

held. We had no clue as to the layout of the property. I didn't know what Pandora looked like. We also had no idea how many flaming assholes were there to protect her. For all I knew, Abaddon was dead.

My mother had been right. I had no inkling of what I was about to deal with. However, I wasn't going to quit. I needed to call her again and beg for help. Granted, she'd said she was sending people. Abaddon might already be back in LA...

I was a colossal idiot. I'd been aware of my Demon status for barely a week. Who did I think I was to take on the Goddess Pandora?

"This isn't going to work," I said, banging my head on the steering wheel.

"Whoa, Nelly! I beg to differ," Cher shouted, causing me to wince. "Where's that twenty-year-old girl who knew she could fly?"

"Right here," I said with my head still on the steering wheel. "She has a few teeth implants and a scar on her forehead to prove it. It's not possible for a human to fly. Period."

"Bad attitude," Ophelia informed me.

I glanced over at her and made a face. "You're a fine one to talk about attitude."

She shrugged and lifted her middle finger. "Just stating the obvious, bitch."

I was so close to waving my fingers and singeing all the blonde hair off her head. I didn't. I really, *really* wanted to, but she'd made a halfway decent point. It wasn't about flying at all. It was about believing. But, believing I could rescue Abaddon and defeat Pandora by doing an *act* with Ophelia could lose me more than just teeth.

Cher was still in her own warped world. "I've got it! And

there's very little to no nudity involved. We can make that part optional."

"I'm fine with a little tit," Ophelia stated.

"I'm not," I ground out.

"No worries. We can do it without a display of the knockers! Does anyone do rope tricks?"

Ophelia shook her head. I just rolled my eyes.

Cher tried yet again. "Ventriloquism?"

"Seriously?" I choked out on a semi-hysterical laugh.

"I don't know what that means, so I'm going with a no," Ophelia told us.

My agent would not give up. That was great in contract negotiations, but not great right now. The ideas kept getting worse.

"Can either of you do magic tricks?" she asked.

"No," I said flatly, not waiting to hear what Ophelia had to offer on the subject.

"Not so fast," the Demon chimed in. "I mean, Cecily could saw me in half at the midsection then show my bloody innards to the audience. The shock value would go over well with that crowd. Then once the curtain comes down, Cher can heal me."

Cher patted Ophelia on the back. "I like the way you think."

"Oh my God," I shouted. "I am not sawing Ophelia in half. First off, it's all kinds of wrong. Secondly, I'd puke. Not sure that would go over too well."

Cher shrugged. "Gotta disagree with you, Cecily. The puking is genius. Makes it real. Probably would get a few laughs too."

I shook my head instead of shaking the two women in my truck. Was everyone insane?

"We have to get in another way," I explained. "It's not like we can walk into the place, march up onto the main stage and start maiming each other."

"Actually, we could," Ophelia said. "However, Cecily has a good point. I think if she hacked me in two and then hurled, we'd be very popular. Might be difficult to find Abaddon if people are constantly asking for autographs and pics."

"I see what you mean." Cher penciled in her already-penciled eyebrows. "How about you gals pole dance in a cage above the crowd? Pretty sure I have some baby oil in my bag. If not, I've definitely got lube. The over twelve-million-year-old vagina needs it. We can grease you up good. You could suss out the sitch from up there and then make your move when the time is right. Jump out of the cage and kick ass. The grease'll help you get away if some asshole tries to grab you. Ophelia can distract the bad guys with her rack and Cecily can whip out her purple fire sword and lop some heads off. I'll grab Abaddon while you two make sure that Rhoda Spark gets her ass handed to her and then we'll leave. We'll be back in time to work on Monday. Bingo, bango, bongo!"

Yep. Everyone was insane.

"No," I said quietly. "The goal is to save Abaddon. I'm worried we're going to get him killed. I have to call my mom."

"Your mom?" Cher asked, confused. "I thought she was dead."

"Metaphorically speaking, she is," I told her. "Literally speaking, she's not."

"She's a high-ranking Demon?" Ophelia asked, just as perplexed as Cher. "A powerful Demon that can help?"

I nodded and opened up the door. "Give me a sec. And while I'm gone, think of another plan, please."

The walk across the rutted parking lot felt like an eternity. The strip mall was rundown and shoddy. I almost tripped on the crumbling asphalt as I put some distance between the women in my truck and me. I'd come close to telling Cher and Ophelia who my mother was, but held back. I wasn't sure that was fair to them, but something told me not to share too much, too soon.

A single streetlamp illuminated the area where I stood. It was rusted out and had a few bullet holes in it. Nice. I glanced around for people, but it was truly deserted. Even the stars hanging low in the sky and bathing the lot in a sparkling glow couldn't disguise the dilapidated and sad conditions.

I dialed the number.

She answered on the first ring. She was out of breath and sounded distracted.

"Lilith?" I asked, not sure I'd gotten the right number. I regretted eating the card.

"Yes, hold on a moment, please," she replied. "Just need to behead a few people."

"Right," I muttered. I supposed when your mother was a Demon Goddess, this was a normal conversation.

I waited a few minutes. I heard screams and a few thuds. My gut roiled. It would be all kinds of karmically screwed if I was on the phone with her when she bit the dust. Holding my breath, I sent good juju out into the Universe that she would successfully decapitate whoever was in her way.

"I'm back," she announced triumphantly. "Are you in LA?"

"No," I told her. "I'm a few miles from the Golden Showers Bet and Bed. Are you there?"

"You're very disobedient, Cecily," Lilith reprimanded me.

"Thank you. Answer my question."

"Yes, I'm outside of the casino," she replied in a clipped tone.

"Did you find Abaddon?"

She sighed. "Yes and no. Pandora has him and she's well protected."

"Are you?" I asked as my stomach tightened in fear. She wouldn't be there if I hadn't said I was going. If she died before I met her, I'd be devastated. Every move I made lately was a mess.

"Am I what?" she asked.

"Protected," I answered.

Her laugh had a quality that made me feel whole and warm. It was ridiculous, but I didn't know how else to describe it.

"You care?" she inquired.

"Irrelevant," I replied coolly. "Just answer the question."

"I'm protected. I'm also in disguise," she shared. "Rumor has it that Pandora will be attending a concert with her new lover Abaddon tomorrow night. That will be our best chance at getting him back safely."

The fact that the words lover, Pandora, and Abaddon had been used in the same sentence made me want to set something on fire. I didn't. I didn't believe for one second that he was her new lover. However, if we got there and I was proven wrong, I'd electrocute him and leave.

"Where's the concert?" I asked, hoping it wasn't at a venue filled with humans.

"Here. At the Golden Showers Casino. I can't even begin to imagine who named this dump." She was quiet for a beat then spoke. "As much as it pains me to say it, I do believe there's a way for you to be of use, Cecily."

The feeling of pride that welled up inside me was absurd. My mother was the Demon Goddess Lilith. The fact that she wanted my help felt glorious. Until it didn't.

"Tell me first who you're with," she said.

"Ophelia. She's a Demon," I told her.

"I know her. Ophelia is loyal to me. She can be trusted," she replied. "Is your father with you?"

The tone of her voice was wistful. It infuriated me. She didn't deserve to feel anything for either of us. Lilith had dumped us a long time ago.

"No. He's not. I wouldn't risk him like that," I said curtly. "My agent Cher is with me. She's an Angel."

"I don't know an Angel named Cher," she said. "Is she powerful?"

I heaved out a sigh. "Not sure how to answer that. I didn't even know Angels existed until earlier today. She did heal Ophelia after Rhoda Spark tried to kill her then kidnapped Abaddon."

"About that," Lilith said, sounding perplexed. "How was Rhoda able to take Abaddon? She's nowhere near his power."

"Well," I said, pacing the parking lot, "my Uncle Grim Fucking Reaper did a little voodoo on me to help me control my magic after I almost killed myself, my brother and my dad. Abaddon took the pain for me and almost died. He's apparently at half a tank for a day."

"That wouldn't kill him. Very unusual, though. He must care for you," she muttered, clearly taking in what I'd just said. "When did he lose strength?"

"Late this afternoon."

"Perfect. He'll be restored by the time we get him out. So, as I said, I believe you can help."

"How?" I asked.

"We need backstage passes to the concert in order to infiltrate and surround the casino without anyone catching on. I'll need twenty at the minimum. Thirty would be better."

I had no clue how I could help her with that. "Not sure I can make that happen."

"Ahh, but you can, child," she replied. "You know the lead singer of the band."

"Umm... my guess is that you're aware that I'm in show business, but I'm not in the cool kids' club. I don't hang out with rock stars."

"But you do know Slash Gordon."

"Shit," I said with a shudder. Yes... I unfortunately knew my ex-husband. "Slash Gordon is the headliner at the Golden Showers Bet and Bed?" Honestly, I didn't know why that surprised me at all. It was fitting.

"Bingo. I need you to get the passes. Are you still friendly with the man?"

"Friendly would be pushing it," I admitted. "But he reached out recently."

"Excellent. It will end up being far less bloody if we don't have to storm the casino. Will you make the call?"

"I can and I will," I said, trying not to gag. I had no clue what the jackass would want in return, but this wasn't about me. It was about Abaddon.

Lilith was all business. "Stay away from the casino until the concert. You will give me the passes and then leave," she said in a brook-no-bullshit tone. "Don't be a hero, Cecily. It will not end well. Pandora is vicious and has very little conscience. It's under debate if she's aware of who you are, but as heinous as she is, she's very smart. She will not hesitate to end you. Am I clear?"

"You're clear, Lilith," I replied. I'd heard every word she'd just said. I took none of it lightly. The passes would be obtained. I didn't know how yet, but if I could fly, I could get twenty to thirty damn backstage passes from the jackass who I'd been married to for a short stint a very long time ago.

As for not helping to save the man who was the reason I

was still standing at the moment, I wasn't on board. There was going to be a bounty on my head for the rest of my life. Being a danger to Man-mom and Sean was unacceptable. If I went down in a blaze of glory saving the person who was beginning to mean something important to me, then so be it. While Lilith's concern was nice, it had come far too late.

And I hadn't lied to her either. I'd acknowledged she was clear. I didn't say I would obey.

"The concert starts at eight," she went on. "I'll meet you in the parking lot at seven."

"What do you look like?" I asked, feeling ridiculous.

She laughed. "I look very much like you, Cecily."

I closed my eyes and willed myself not to fall into the magic of her laugh. It was hard. "You said you were in disguise," I reminded her in a harsh tone.

"I'll remove it momentarily for you, child," she whispered. "Stay safe."

She hung up and I swiped at my angry tears. Crying would solve nothing. I'd already cried for years over her. I'd spent thousands in therapy trying to figure out why she didn't love me. Lilith didn't deserve any more of my tears.

I had a job to do and I was going to do it.

No. I wasn't just going to do it. I was going to fly.

And this time, I had no plans to face plant.

CHAPTER FIVE

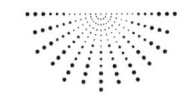

When I left the truck, there were two women inside it.

When I came back, there were three.

Call me incredibly confused…

I didn't say a single word. I waited for them to explain themselves. Not only did I know the new woman in the car, I considered her a friend. This otherworldly crap was freaking me out.

"Came up with another plan," Cher announced with a wink.

I just nodded.

"Wanna hear it?"

I glanced over at Ophelia, who looked amused. Then I turned and stared at the two grinning fools in the back.

One in particular.

It was Sushi—just Sushi. No last name I was aware of. Pretty sure it wasn't the name she was born with, but who was I to judge? I'd worked with Sushi a bunch over the years on TV shows and movies. I'd just hired her as head costume designer for my new sitcom because she was brilliant, along with my dear friend Jenni as the makeup head. Sushi looked like a very well-preserved sixty-year-old, blunt and all business, who enjoyed wearing low-cut tops that showed off her enviable assets. However, her assets had increased since I'd seen her last week. She was now more than a double D. It broke my heart what women in Hollywood thought they had to do to stay relevant. And Sushi was behind the damn camera for the love of everything unnecessary.

In her youth she must have been beautiful. What she lacked in the social graces department, she made up for in talent, professionalism and a sarcastic sense of humor.

"Sushi, would you like to explain why and how you're in my truck right now?" I asked.

"Sure thing," she said with a thumbs up. "Cher texted me that she needed catering uniforms ASAP so I brought them."

"Right," I said, wondering how many freaking people in my life were not who I thought they were. "And you drove here in five minutes?"

Sushi threw her head back and laughed. Cher joined her. Even Ophelia chuckled.

I didn't.

Shaking my head, I decided to get right to the heart of the matter. "Are you human?"

"Nope."

I tried again. "Are you a Demon?"

Sushi shook her head. "Not a Demon."

I had a fifty-fifty chance of getting it correct. I should have gone with Angel first.

"So, you're an Angel," I said.

"Not an Angel," Sushi said, grinning.

I narrowed my eyes at her. She chuckled.

"If you're not human, Angel or Demon, what are you?"

"Guess, Cecily Bloom," she challenged.

Her eyes were literally twinkling. It was bizarre. Although, I was one to talk. I had Goat Eyes.

"Umm... a fairy?"

"No such thing as fairies," Cher chimed in.

"Fine," I muttered. "How old are you?"

"Rude," Sushi pointed out.

"Under normal circumstances, yes," I admitted. "The circumstances are not normal."

Sushi raised a brow. "Ten thousand."

I closed my eyes briefly. Ask stupid questions, get stupid answers. However, I was pretty sure she was telling the truth. Cher was twelve million years old.

"Alien?" I guessed.

"Are you serious?" Ophelia asked with an enormous eye roll.

"I don't know," I snapped. "I didn't know any of this shit existed a week ago. If there are Angels and Demons, why in the heck wouldn't there be aliens?"

"Good guess," Sushi said. "But no."

"A witch?" I asked, thinking that was a real possibility.

"Literally or figuratively?" Sushi shot back.

"Literally."

Sushi was enjoying herself way too much for my sanity. "No, but I've been called a witch many times."

"A vampire?" I asked with a wince.

"No."

I kept going. "Werewolf?"

"Nope."

"What else is there?" I asked, bewildered.

"You're a dumbass," Ophelia muttered.

"Screw you," I snapped at her. "How about instead of sitting there like a useless pain in my butt, you help me out?"

For dramatic effect, she lifted both middle fingers and aimed them at me.

"Are you fond of your hair?" I asked her.

"I am, bitch," she replied, yanking off her shirt and wrapping it around her head.

Not the result I was looking for.

"Put your shirt back on and give me a hint," I told her.

Warily, she pulled it back over her head. "Fine. Here's a hint. If you're not good…"

"You're bad," I replied.

"No."

I rolled my eyes. "Yes, the opposite of good is bad."

"Lemme try," Cher said. "If someone is really, really, really bad at something, they…"

I racked my brain. "Umm… they stink. Sushi is a skunk shifter?"

Ophelia blew a raspberry. Sushi and Cher giggled.

Cher patted my shoulder. "When you give a blow job, you…"

"Are we really going there?" I asked with a groan.

"It's a very good clue in so many ways," Sushi said, defending my agent.

"Fine. The answer is, you suck."

"Bingo!" Cher shouted. "Now guess what Sushi is!"

"An Immortal hooker?" I asked.

"So close," Sushi said in an encouraging tone. "You've got this! Try again."

"Another hint," I requested.

"How did you get to school when you were young?" Cher asked.

"I walked," I said, trying to put it together. I didn't actually go to regular school because of *Camp Bite*, but if I had, it was right down the street from our old house in the Valley. "Is Sushi an Immortal streetwalker?"

Sushi cackled. Cher whipped out hard ciders and passed them around.

I was so confused. "Did I get it right?"

"No. You're beginning to sound as stupid as you look," Ophelia said. "If school was too far away for a kid to walk, they took the…"

"Bus." I mulled the clues around in my head, then choked on my cider. "Holy shit! Sushi is a Succubus?"

"Ding, ding, ding!" Sushi said. "I'm a Succubus."

"So… you eat your lovers?" I asked.

"Myth," she explained. "Succubi do not eat their lovers. We drain them of their life force during sex. Sirens, on the other hand, ingest their paramours after orgasm. The Succubi method is far less messy."

But no less horrifying.

"Do you do that a lot?" I asked, not wanting the answer but needing to know. I didn't want to fire her from the show, but if she offed any of the crew or cast that would not be good.

"Do I do what?" Sushi asked.

"Umm… suck the life force out of your lovers," I replied.

Sushi laughed like I'd just told a hilarious joke. I didn't think any of it was funny.

"Gave that up nine centuries ago," she explained. "Got tired of having to bury bodies. Came close to getting busted one time and decided the big O wasn't worth getting hunted for life. Considering I have a very long life it wouldn't be all that fun."

"Wow," I said, unable to come up with anything more eloquent.

"So, you don't bang anymore?" Ophelia asked, fascinated.

I was kind of curious too, but never would have asked.

"Masturbation is the name of the game," Sushi shared, pulling a mini vibrator out of her pocket and showing us. "I can get myself off quicker than any man ever could and no one dies. Win-win."

Not to be one-upped, Cher pulled her own vibrator out of her bag. The conversation had taken a hard left and was now in the *I really didn't want to know* territory.

"So smart to carry your pleasure toys with you," Ophelia said, impressed. "I'll start doing that too. It'll save me from banging idiots and assholes."

"Word," Cher said. "If it wasn't for my BOB I'd probably get married again."

"How many times have you been hitched?" Sushi asked her.

Cher's brow wrinkled in thought. She was quiet for a full five minutes while she tried to figure it out. I almost laughed. She was twelve million years old after all…

"Hell's bells," she said with a giggle. "I'm not sure. Anyhoo, back to the new plan."

"Plans have changed," I told all of them. "My mother had an idea."

"Thought your mom was dead," Sushi said, looking confused.

"Meteorically, yes," Ophelia said. "Litteringly, she's not."

I winced at her painful misuse of the English language but didn't correct her. Sushi seemed to get it and also didn't comment.

"Is it better than going in as caterers and poisoning Pandora? So that when she gets the explosive shits, we sneak in and abscond with Abaddon?" Cher inquired.

"Substantially better," I told her.

"Let's hear it!" Cher bellowed with glee.

THE EDGE OF EVIL

I blew out a long, slow, strained breath. "Do you have Slash Gordon's number? His direct number?"

Cher grabbed her phone and scrolled. "Dammit, I only have his manager's digits. I'm sure I could get it, though."

"I have it," Ophelia offered up. "Banged him a few times. He's an asshole. Why do you want his number? If you want to get laid, I have way better numbers you can have than his. I've banged 'em all."

I wasn't remotely jealous that she'd banged my ex. The news was gross. And while her offer was nice in a screwed-up way, I did *not* want Ophelia's sloppy seconds. "Not looking to get laid," I said, doing my best not to gag. "I need backstage passes to his concert tomorrow night."

"Sounds to me like you want to bang the douchebag," Ophelia commented.

I rolled my eyes. "I was married to the disgusting douchebag for five minutes. Trust me, I do *not* want to bang him. Been there, done that. Not going back."

The Demon wrinkled her nose. "Ewwww."

"Correct," I said. "Complete and total ewww."

It was a pleasant if not somewhat disturbing bonding moment with Ophelia.

Cher looked a bit worried and began to line her lips with a black eye pencil. I took it away from her.

"Spit out the plan before Cher starts using permanent markers on her face," Sushi suggested.

It was a good idea.

So, I did.

I told them the plan. I added every detail except my mother's name. That would be revealed only if necessary.

Sushi thought it was brilliant. Cher loved it. Only Ophelia was skeptical.

"Is Lilith aware of what's about to go down?" she inquired.

Holding back my laugh was hard but doable. "Yes. I've been told she knows and is on board."

"Told by?" Ophelia pressed.

"My mother."

"Who is?" the Demon asked.

"Who is not important," I shot back. "The plan is good. We have to find someplace to stay for the night. I'll call Slash in the morning."

"No worries," Sushi said. "I own a club not far from here. The Presidential Suite is always held for me. The suite has four bedrooms and is stocked with the finest champagne and caviar. We'll go there."

"Ohhhh! A club," Ophelia squealed. "Is there gambling?"

"But of course," Sushi replied. "And much more."

"I'm feelin' lucky tonight," Cher crowed.

I hoped she wasn't planning on cheating. I'd have to keep an eye on her. That would be rude considering we were guests.

"Holy cow." I gave Sushi a wide smile. "Thank you."

She winked. "That's what friends are for."

It was seriously good to have friends even if they were hundreds or even thousands of years older than me. I was a lucky gal.

CHAPTER SIX

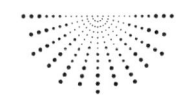

When Sushi had mentioned the Presidential Suite, I thought her place would be swanky. It was. It was very swanky. It was also skanky.

The exterior was not attractive. It was a huge, old, several-story-high warehouse. The phrase "don't judge a book by its cover" bounced around in my head as I parked my pickup between a Mercedes and a Jaguar. It wasn't on the Strip or in Old Vegas. It was in the middle of nowhere. Sushi had given directions since there was no technical street address that would come up on GPS. That alone should have tipped me off, but a beggar couldn't be a chooser. We needed a place to stay and Sushi had volunteered to put us up.

The ragged outsides belied what was inside.

My mouth dropped open as we entered. Cher squealed with delight, and Ophelia adjusted her cleavage so the girls were on better display. Sushi was greeted like she was a dignitary.

The crowd milling around was well dressed in black tie evening wear. The servers—both men and women who were beyond stunning—wore crisp white tuxes and red patent leather shoes. Unusual but it somehow worked. I felt incredibly underdressed.

Champagne flutes atop silver trays and hors d'oeuvres were carried by the staff who seemed to be floating on air as they made their way through the fancy guests. It felt like I'd walked onto the set of a movie or more possibly into the Hotel California, where you could enter but never leave. It was unsettling.

The high-class vibe clashed with the brightly lit, shiny silver, floor-to-ceiling poles that were evenly spread throughout the club. There was one every ten feet as far as the eye could see. Barely clad women and men undulated up and down the poles to the sultry beat coming from hidden speakers. In between were mahogany tables trimmed in red leather where high-stakes card games were being played.

"My kind of joint," Ophelia announced, grabbing a glass of champagne and downing it.

"What is this place?" I whispered to Cher as Sushi warmly greeted people.

"Not sure," Cher said, glancing around. "But it looks like fun!"

"Is anyone here human?" I asked, passing on the champagne.

"Doubtful," Cher said. "Most likely Demons, Angels, regular Immortals and possibly a few Succubi."

I hoped the Succubi present were on the same sex restrictions as Sushi. "What's a regular Immortal?"

"I misspoke," Cher said, slapping on some blush. "Nothin' regular about them. Very powerful. Best to keep a wide berth."

"How do I tell the difference?" I whisper-hissed in her ear. I didn't need to die tonight. I had shit to do.

THE EDGE OF EVIL

"You can't," she explained, swiping a few caviar tarts from a passing server. "Just know that everyone here is most likely insane, deadly and very powerful. Kind of like a Hollywood action blockbuster but with a more permanent ending."

"Awesome," I replied, wondering how rude it would be if I grabbed Cher and Ophelia and looked for a Holiday Inn. They were clean, reasonably priced and not filled with people older than dirt who could off you with the wiggle of a pinkie finger.

"Alrighty," Sushi said, waltzing over and handing each of us a flute of champagne. "The VIP room is in the back. I've requested a meal for us and we'll have privacy."

"Umm… Sushi," I said with a forced smile. "I'm kind of new to all this… you know… stuff. Are we safe here?"

She gave me a quick hug. "Absolutely," Sushi assured me. "Just don't have sex with any of the serving staff. They're all Succubi who are working to overcome that pesky killing thing."

"Wait. Succubi can kill Immortals? I thought it was only humans," I said.

"Succubi are rather unique," she explained. "Best not to mess with them. All terrific folks, but addictions are hard to break. Took me centuries."

"Good to know," Ophelia said. "I won't bang anyone wearing red patent leather shoes."

I rolled my eyes. "We're not here to have sex," I reminded the Demon. "We're here to get some sleep. We have a huge day tomorrow."

Ophelia raised a brow. "Tomorrow may never come, Cecily Bloom. Live for the moment."

"You're attitude sucks," I snapped. "I plan to be here for a while."

My words weren't completely true. I was very aware that

tomorrow might be my last. Just looking around at all the crazy made me surer of my choice to go down swinging. My dad's and brother's lives were on the line due to flaming assholes trying to kill me on the regular. If my loved ones came to harm because of me it would be my worst nightmare.

Tomorrow was definitely coming. I just wasn't as certain about the day after.

"Girls," Cher said. "Let's not ruin a lovely evening filled with so much delightful eye candy! I say we hit the VIP room, eat, play a little roulette then hit the sack."

"Love it," Sushi said, leading us to the back of the club. "There's a special guest waiting there."

None of that sounded right to me. I'd been with all three of the women the entire time in the truck. How was someone aware we were here? Granted, the gals had their phones and could have texted.

I'd crap my pants if they'd poofed Slash Gordon in.

"Tada!" Sushi sang as we left the main area and entered a much smaller but equally formal section.

The chandeliers sparkled gold and reflected off the shiny hardwood floors. Four tables for six were dressed in pristine white linen. The cutlery was definitely real silver and the plates were a shimmering red with flecks of gold. The floral arrangements were blood-red roses… with the thorns still attached. It was over the top.

Thankfully, there was only one pole and I didn't recognize anyone.

The woman straddling the pole was clearly inexperienced. She wore mismatched sweats, tennis shoes and a baseball cap. She had a toothpick hanging out of her mouth. I watched in shock as she hit the floor with a loud thud then cussed up a storm that would have made a sailor blush. She limped around then attempted to get back on the pole.

No one took notice. They just ignored the poor woman. She didn't seem quite right in the head.

Was I in the twilight zone? There were around fifteen people in the VIP area. With the staff it was easily twenty. How was no one worried?

The toothpick-wielding gal was probably Immortal, but that didn't mean she wouldn't end up with a gnarly concussion.

"Fuckin' pole," she grunted as she leapt onto it, only to fall right back off, smacking her head on the floor so hard, I got a phantom headache.

Again, no reaction from anyone.

It was absurd. Plus, to make matters worse, with the toothpick in her mouth she could choke or gouge her esophagus. Without really thinking it through, I quickly walked over to the woman and helped her up.

"Not sure this is your thing," I said, removing the toothpick from her mouth and handing it to her. "But if you insist, you might not want to chew on a piece of wood."

The woman was attractive in a messy way. I'd guess her to be late thirties or maybe early forties. Of course, she was probably a million years old. It amazed me how the Immortals played with their ages. If she brushed her hair and wore clothes that matched even just a little bit, she would look a heck of a lot better.

"And why the fuck not?" she demanded, putting two toothpicks into her mouth.

I tilted my head and tried to decide if she would kill me for honesty. I needed to stay alive until tomorrow night.

I shrugged. "I don't know the Heimlich Maneuver and no one else seems to be real invested."

She threw her head back and laughed. Then, in what I hoped was a friendly move, she slapped me on the back.

I went flying.

"Motherfucker," she yelled as she hustled over and helped me up. "Sorry 'bout that. I forget my strength. You okay, Cecily Bloom?"

I froze. I was positive I hadn't introduced myself. My stomach lurched and did a flip-flop. If she was a Demon who was loyal to Pandora, I was in trouble. Surely, Sushi wouldn't have allowed the enemy in.

"Cat got your tongue, Demon?" she asked, shoving me into a chair at one of the tables. "No worries. I can do the talkin'," the toothpick-wielding woman said. "Just so you know, the food here sucks ass—lots of tiny portions covered in some kind of foamy shit that looks like cat piss. I have some Goobers and Snickers in my pocket. If you get hungry, let me know."

I nodded and plastered what I hoped was a pleasant smile on my face. I had no clue what game we were playing and I still didn't know the rules. The fact that she was here and no one made mention of her attire or her appalling pole skills made me think that she was either really powerful, super crazy, or extremely terrifying.

I'd put my money on all three.

"Candy Vargo?" Cher screamed at the top of her lungs, hightailing it over to the table and bear-hugging the wannabe pole dancer. "What in the hell are you doing here, you batshit crazy old bag?"

"Slummin'. What are you goin' by now, old lady?" Candy Vargo asked with a grin. "Last time I saw you it was Queen Victoria."

"Right, that was my royalty phase," Cher said with a chuckle. "Gave that crap up when I started going by Ann Boleyn and almost got myself decapitated. That was around the time you ran over Tim with a chariot and chopped off his legs."

"Good times." Candy Vargo laughed.

Cher laughed.

I didn't really understand what was so funny about amputation. I seriously hoped Tim was Immortal and grew his legs back. I was tempted to ask, but didn't really want the answer. Either way it was awful.

"Those were really good times," Candy Vargo said, offering my agent a toothpick.

She took it, sat down next to me, then pulled Candy down next to her. "I go by Cher now. Thinking about changing it to Adele or maybe Rihanna. I bore so easily."

I wondered if she even remembered her real name. Out of curiosity, I made a mental note to ask.

My insane agent pulled out her makeup bag and went to town on her buddy's face. While the crowd didn't seem phased by Candy Vargo's pole dancing debacle, they all gasped in terror when Cher began to slap war paint onto her face.

One by one, the VIPs slipped out of the room. Some of them ran. Even the staff skedaddled. The only people left were Cher, Sushi, Ophelia, me and Candy Vargo.

Cher was having a field day. Candy was sporting so much lipliner she could have passed for a clown. My agent was heavy-handed with cosmetics.

Sushi was highly amused.

Ophelia was a little green around the gills and looked like she wanted to make a run for it. It was the first time I was in total agreement with the Demon.

Candy Vargo just gnawed on her toothpick and bitched.

"Works like a dream every time," Cher said with a giggle, handing her friend a package of makeup wipes from her bottomless bag.

"What works like a dream?" I asked.

"Candy Vargo isn't one to wear makeup," Cher explained. "No one in their right mind would ever attempt something as foolish as gussying up the old bag without having a death wish!"

"I'm so lost," I said, ready to escape if necessary.

"They want privacy," Ophelia whispered, slowly backing away in the direction of the door.

Her move made me nervous. There were a lot of unanswered questions with potentially nausea-inducing answers. Why was Candy Vargo here? Why did she know my name? Who in the hell was she? And why did she think pole dancing was a good plan?

My gut said that Ophelia had a fine idea, but my head said I needed to stay. Stuff seemed to happen for a reason lately. My stomach felt wonky and I was exhausted. I was surrounded by insanity. Life was so much easier when I was getting fired from sitcoms and hanging with Man-mom, Dead Uncle Joe, and Sean. Learning I was a Demon had turned my world upside down.

I didn't have time to run and hide. If this Candy Vargo person was batshit crazy that was her problem. Not mine. I just needed to know why she'd shown up and if it had anything to do with me.

"Question," I announced, running my hand through my hair and hoping I'd see the light of day in the morning... which wasn't all that far off. "Who are you? Why are you here? And why do you know my name? If you're here to kill me, let me know so I can get a few good shots in before I bite it. I'm new to this and would like to be prepared."

Sushi's brows rose high. Ophelia sank to her knees and crawled under a table. Cher's mouth formed a perfect O. None of the signs were good. I stood up and reached deep for stuff that pissed me off. My hardcore power seemed to come from anger.

Candy Vargo removed her toothpick and rose to her feet. She began to glow. It was terrifying.

Slowly, she approached me. "You've got some big balls, motherfucker."

I stood my ground. "Thank you."

"You think you can take me?" she inquired with a grin that would visit me in my nightmares.

"Nope, but I won't go down without a fight, motherfucker," I shot right back.

My bravado was going to end me, but I would not die without getting a few electrocutions in.

Candy Vargo threw her head back and laughed. She laughed so hard, I thought she would choke on her toothpick. Right now, that might not be a bad thing. If she was choking, I might be able to take her out. Highly unlikely, but it was a maybe.

"You done?" I asked as she wiped away tears.

"Nope, and neither are you with that badass attitude," she said with a chuckle.

She sat back down at the table and patted the chair next to her. I warily walked over and accepted the invitation.

"Everybody out of here," she said. "This is a conversation between me and Big Balls."

Cher didn't look worried at all. That gave me the confidence to believe I wasn't going to be dead in the next five minutes. Sushi dragged Ophelia from under the table and out of the door. My agent kissed the top of my head and winked at the certifiable Candy Vargo.

"Cecily, listen to what the Keeper of Fate has to say," she advised as she put her makeup case back in her bag and slung it onto her shoulder. "The old hag is nuts, but she's smart."

One question answered. Candy Vargo was the Keeper of Fate. I wasn't sure what that meant, but I had a pretty good idea.

I wasn't necessarily a believer in fate. I was more of a make-your-own-fate kind of gal. However, until last week I didn't believe in Demons. Maybe fate was predestined. Maybe Bigfoot was real…

As my agent left the VIP area, she grabbed a bottle of champagne and waved goodbye.

I was alone with the toothpick-loving Candy Vargo. As I stared at her, something clicked in my brain and I held back my bile with effort. I was pretty sure I was sitting with the woman Cher had spoken of earlier. The Angel-eating Immortal. My gut roiled.

Closing my eyes, I decided to just get it out of the way. There was no way I could take in what she had to tell me if I was picturing her eating people. Hopefully, Cher had a lot of toothpick-loving buddies.

"Did you eat the Angels?" I asked, getting right into it.

"For the love of everything fuckin' none of your business," she groused, shaking her head.

"Did you?" I asked.

She sighed dramatically. "Yes, I did. They had it coming after attacking and dismembering me. But not to worry, I crapped them out and they're fine. I'd call them semi-friendly fuckin' acquaintances now."

I squinted at her in shock. "How is that possible?"

She shrugged. "Don't know. Don't care. If you play stupid games, you win stupid fuckin' prizes."

"Got it," I said, reminding myself not to mess with her. Ever. Getting eaten then crapped out wasn't on my bucket list. "Do you still eat people?"

She rolled her eyes. "Fuck no. It was disgusting. Wouldn't have done it if they hadn't chopped off all my appendages. Didn't leave me too many choices."

I took that in and mulled it over. I was ninety-nine percent sure I wasn't about to get eaten. I had no intention of lopping off her arms and legs. Would I eat flaming assholes if it was me or them? No. However, I refused to judge the insane woman. Pushing the graphic images out of my head, I moved on. What she'd done in the past—no matter how repulsive and physically unfathomable—was not my business. Why she was here now apparently *was* my business.

"Why do you know who I am?"

Candy Vargo pulled out a box of toothpicks and placed them on the table. She took three and put them in her mouth then nodded at me.

Fine. When in Rome… I took four.

She grinned.

I grinned right back. It was strangely comforting to chew on wood. Who knew?

"Known about you since the day you were born," she replied. "Been watchin' you, Cecily Bloom."

"Because?" I pressed.

"Because you hold the balance of the Darkness in your hands."

My heart sped up and I felt a little faint. "Do you see the future?"

Candy Vargo chuckled. "I do. However, free will can change it on a dime."

"What do you see?" I asked.

I'd never been one to go to psychics or mediums. There were plenty of people in Hollywood who kept their psychic on speed dial and visited them more than their plastic surgeon. I did not. I preferred to let life kick my ass without watching it come at me due to prior knowledge. Although, I did like to read my horoscope.

I held up my hand. "Wait. Don't answer that."

"Smart fuckin' cookie," she replied pulling some squished-looking candy bars out of her pocket and offering me one.

"I'm good," I told her. "While I don't want my future told, I'm guessing it's not an accident you're here."

She shoved the full-sized Snickers into her mouth then proceeded to speak. I had to subtly dodge the peanuts that were flying out of her mouth.

"There were two. Now there are three." She wiped her mouth with the back of her hand. "Three's a fuckin' crowd."

I inhaled deeply. She was referring to Lilith, Pandora and me. Was she foretelling my death? If the ridiculous prophecy that the Demons seemed to believe had come true with my birth, then I was a sitting duck. "I prefer, *Three's Company*. Much funnier."

The Keeper of Fate grinned. "Gideon and Daisy were right."

"You know them?" I asked. Did all freaking Immortals know each other?

"You could say that," she replied. "Remember this, anger will eat you alive."

"Umm… like literally?" I asked. I mean, Candy Vargo seemed to have cannibalistic tendencies… maybe she knew something I didn't.

"Fuck no," she said with a bellow of laughter. "Let me rephrase. According to Buddha, 'Holding on to anger is like grasping a hot coal with the intent of throwing it at someone else; you are the one who gets burned.'"

I sighed. Cryptic wasn't going to work. "Do you have anything more solid? Like how to get Abaddon back?"

She stared at me for a long beat. I held her gaze.

"So nice to be around people who aren't terrified of me," she commented.

"Should I be?" I questioned.

"Yep. But to answer your question, I don't know."

"Awesome," I muttered. "Is there anything more?"

"There's always more," she replied. "Try this one on for size, 'Forgiveness is not an occasional act, it is a constant attitude.'"

"Martin Luther King Jr.," I said automatically. Due to the games Man-mom, Sean and I played while growing up, I could throw quotes around like a pro. "How'd we get from anger to forgiveness?"

"Natural fuckin' progression," she explained. "'The weak can never forgive. Forgiveness is the attribute of the strong.'"

"Mahatma Gandhi," I said.

"One more," Candy Vargo said with a grin. "'Always forgive your enemies—nothing annoys them so much.'"

"Oscar Wilde," I said. "All of this applies to me?"

She stood up and put three more toothpicks into her mouth. "Only if you choose to let it."

As she went to grab the box of toothpicks on the table, I put my hand on hers. "Can I have them?"

Her grin was so wide it had to have hurt her face. "My fuckin' pleasure, Big Balls. Stay true, follow your gut and trust your power. Remember that people with more experience tend to make better decisions than people who don't, and being a martyr is bullshit."

I gave her a hug. "Thank you, Candy Vargo," I told her, not quite sure what all that meant, but committing it to memory. I was excellent at memorization due to being an actress my entire life.

She awkwardly patted my back then pulled away. "Loved that *Camp Bite* show, Cecily Bloom. You fought the bad guy and always won."

"That was fiction."

"'Truth is stranger than fiction, but it is because fiction is obliged to stick to possibilities; Truth isn't.'"

"Mark Twain," I said. "So, the truth has no possibilities?"

"Opposite," she corrected me. "I prefer to interpret that the truth just has stranger fuckin' possibilities. Every motherfucker needs to think outside the box." Candy Vargo checked her watch. "Gotta run. Time change and all," she said. "My foster kids need to wake up for school. Can't be late."

"I'm sorry, what?" I asked, completely confused. She had foster kids?

"Never mind," she said. "Remember what I said. It will all apply eventually, Big Balls."

And on that note, the pole-dancing, Angel-eating, toothpick-loving Keeper of Fate disappeared in a blast of bright lemony-yellow shimmering mist.

I tucked the box of toothpicks into my pocket and sighed. "Anger, bad. Forgiveness, good. Strange fucking possibilities is the way to go. Martyrs are bullshit."

The truth was indeed way stranger than fiction could ever be.

CHAPTER SEVEN

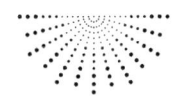

The Presidential Suite was glorious.

As lovely as it was, I'd slept poorly under sheets with a thread count so high I couldn't even guess how much they'd cost. I'd tossed and turned. My mind raced with thoughts of Abaddon—naked and very naughty thoughts. At first, he was the Demon I loved to hate. Now, he might be the Demon I'd hate to love. But more likely, he'd be the Demon I'd love to love and it would blow up in my face like all my other relationships. My track record with men sucked. Adding a Demon who went by the nickname *Destroyer* to my list of failed romances was par for the course.

It didn't matter. Abaddon had saved me. He'd gotten taken because of me. I was going to make sure he was safe. In a short amount of time, the Demon had come to mean more to me than any other man I'd ever been attracted to. That fact probably meant I was as insane as Candy Vargo. Whatever. Dealing with my ex-husband to get backstage passes was nothing compared to the fear of losing Abaddon.

Before Cher, Ophelia, Sushi and I had hit the sack, we'd

eaten delicious mushroom-Swiss hamburgers and truffle fries. I'd shared most of Candy's and my conversation. I left out who my mother was and that I was her daughter who could bring on the prophesized shitshow.

Ophelia was loyal to Lilith. I had no clue how she would feel about me being Lilith's daughter. Clearly, I posed a threat to everyone—including the woman who bore me. Everything would be revealed when and if necessary. Top of the necessary list was saving Abaddon.

What the future held? I had no clue.

After the sleepless night, the morning dawned bright and sunny and had come entirely too fast. However, the breakfast spread in our suite was impressive—fluffy pancakes, eggs with chives and gruyere cheese, bacon, avocado toast with a balsamic drizzle, fresh fruit, coffee, a variety of teas and, of course, mimosas. The Succubi had a thing for champagne.

"You gonna eat that bacon, Cecily?" Cher asked.

My agent looked like a raccoon. It was a terrifying sight this early in the morning. She'd forgotten to remove her eye makeup before bed. Or maybe this was how she always looked in the morning.

"Have at it." I pushed the plate across the table. It was equally as formal as the one in the VIP room, starched white tablecloth and all.

While it was interesting to visit such a fancy place, I could never live this way. If someone had such over-the-top riches around them all of the time, what would there be left to dream about? Although, I'd never dreamt of obscene wealth. I'd dreamt of having a mom…

And now I had one. Kind of.

"When are you going to call the asshole for the passes?" Ophelia inquired, snapping me back into reality.

The Demon was wearing a barely there bra and a thong. She'd walked out of her room to eat breakfast in her birthday suit. Cher had sent her packing and told her to put something on. She'd obeyed for the most part.

Sushi had rushed off in a tizzy right as breakfast was served. Apparently, there was a slight *mishap* with one of the Succubi and a wasted Angel. Thankfully, no one died.

I sipped my coffee and marveled at what my life had become. "I'm going to get caffeinated then make the call."

"Good thinking," Cher said, catching her reflection in the ornate silver teapot.

She screamed.

"Holy shit!" She reached into her bag and pulled out makeup wipes. "Might have been nice if someone had pointed out I look like the Hamburglar in a pink power suit."

I laughed. In the midst of being scared for Abaddon, uncomfortable about calling Slash, feeling angry about seeing Lilith later today and knowing there was a good chance of me biting the dust this evening, my agent could make life seem normal. I adored the silly woman.

"You'd need a black and white striped suit with a cape to complete the look," I told her, picking at some fruit. I wasn't hungry, but knew I needed to eat.

"Like this?" Cher asked with a grin as she snapped her fingers.

With a loud pop and a puff of white glitter, my agent was dressed from head to toe as the Hamburglar.

It was Ophelia's turn to scream. I had to admit it was kind of alarming. The outfit was at least two sizes too small.

"Parlor tricks," Cher said with a chuckle as she snapped her fingers again and dressed herself in a purple power suit and black Prada stilettos. The suit was only one size too small.

"Can you dress me?" Ophelia asked. "If we're going to the Golden Showers Bet and Bed, we'll need to fit in."

"What exactly does that mean?" I asked, topping off my coffee and adding four teaspoons of sugar.

"Black, expensive, lowcut, preferably backless and sky-high stilettos," Ophelia replied.

That didn't sound good to me. The thought of meeting Lilith for the first time dressed like a hooker was embarrassing.

"On it," Cher said, snapping her fingers again.

The pop was loud. The glitter got in my coffee. Ophelia and I were now sporting the *look*.

I glanced down and gulped. My girls were on display and the side boob was abundant. "Seriously?"

"Very," Ophelia said, admiring herself in the mirror. "Versace?"

"But of course," Cher confirmed. "Only the best for my clients."

I sighed and absently added a few more sugars to my sparkling cup of java. Taking a sip, I choked and spit it out.

"This feels wonky," I said, secretly admiring the shoes. They were killer.

"Think of it as an acting role and the dress as your costume," Cher suggested, waving her hand and dressing herself in a designer black power suit with a red sequined corset underneath. "If we're going to play with the big boys we need to be dressed for success."

I poured a fresh cup of coffee and played a card that I didn't intend to use for myself. "We're not going into the casino," I reminded the women. "We're dropping off the passes and staying in the wings, so to speak."

"Boring," Ophelia complained.

Cher shook her head and began to apply green eyeshadow without a mirror. It wasn't going well. "Maybe so, but it's wise to be prepared even if we're not in the thick of it. Pandora is a cow-bitch from Hades. But if Cecily's mom is as powerful as advertised, then we need to follow the advice."

I nodded. I loved Cher to the moon and back. Ophelia was growing on me. Granted she was like an annoying rash, but still... I didn't want either of them in harm's way.

"I'm going to make the call," I said, glancing down at the number Ophelia had supplied. "No one says a word. Got it?"

"Confused," Ophelia said, popping the cork on a bottle of champagne and taking a swig. "We're just going to be silent and prank the asshole? That doesn't seem smart. If you're going to prank him, at least ask if his refrigerator is running."

"Or if he keeps Prince Albert in a can," Cher added with a wink.

I rolled my eyes. I knew Cher was joking. I knew Ophelia was not.

"New plan," I announced, standing up. "I'm going to my room to make the call."

"Good thinking," Ophelia commented. "It might be humiliating to have phone sex in public."

I considered throwing the silver platter of scrambled eggs at her. Refraining was difficult. Instead, I pulled one of her moves out of my bag of tricks. Slowly and deliberately, I flipped the idiot off.

She laughed.

Next time I'd throw the eggs.

"I will *not* be having any kind of sex with Slash Gordon," I informed her flatly. "I'll just ask for the passes. If he's a jerk about it, I'll remind him of our past and guilt him into it."

"People like Slash Gordon don't have much of a

conscience," Cher pointed out. "Might want to go for more of a blackmail angle."

"I'll keep that in mind," I said, walking into my room and closing the door behind me.

Phone sex with a narcissistic jerk, guilt trips and blackmail were not my thing. I prided myself on ethical behavior, which was challenging since I worked in show business. However, this wasn't about me. This was about keeping blood, guts and death to a minimum. Lilith had stated that it would be a lot less bloody if they could get in and surround Abaddon and Pandora without having to storm the casino. Me having to swallow my pride was a tiny price to pay to keep Abaddon safe and my egg donor alive.

"I can do this," I said, pacing the suite. "It's just another role. I'm an actress. I'm a good actress. I can fly. I have the scar and teeth implants to prove it."

I dialed the number three times and couldn't bring myself to press send. My stomach cramped and my head began to ache. It felt as if I was erasing years of therapy by reaching out and asking for something from someone who had crushed me. Yes, I was able to make jokes about having been married for five minutes, but the truth was I'd loved him. After spending thousands upon thousands of dollars to get my head straight, I realized that I was in love with loving someone, and that I'd chosen a man who wasn't capable of loving me back.

"What is wrong with me?" I whispered, pressing my temples and willing my headache to go away. "Slash Gordon is nothing except a reminder of how idiotic and desperate I was in my twenties. He's my past. I'm my future. I'm not young and dumb anymore."

"No, you're old and stupid," Ophelia said, walking into the room and flopping down on the unmade bed.

"Out," I snapped, pointing to the door.

"In a sec," she replied.

I waited. And waited. And waited. The Demon just stared at me. I didn't have time to be analyzed by someone who had bigger boobs than brains.

"Do you have something helpful to say?" I finally asked. She annoyed me, but I had to admit she'd dropped a few stunning truth bombs here and there.

She eyed me for a long moment. "It's clear that you don't have sisters or a mother."

That was not a stunning truth bomb. It was a bullshit statement and mean.

"If you don't want me to electrocute you, you need to get out of here. Now," I ground out.

"One—stop warning people about electrocution. It's not a good strategic plan," she explained with an eye roll, ignoring my threat.

The actor must always please her audience and follow direction... I wiggled my fingers and set her on fire.

"Now that's what I'm talking about," Ophelia squealed with a delighted laugh. She waved her hand and put out the flames. "Always strike first, dumbass. There's no winning if you strike second, mostly because you'll already be dead."

I sighed. "Not helping."

"Actually, I am," she replied and kept going. "Love is friendship that has caught fire. It is quiet understanding, mutual confidence, sharing and forgiving. It is loyalty through the good and bad times. It settles for less than perfection and makes allowances for human weakness."

My mouth fell open. I stared at the woman like she'd grown another head. "Did you come up with that?"

"Nope. It's Ann Landers. Read that column for years. Love

her," Ophelia said. "Little sappy for my taste, but you're kind of a sap."

"Thanks," I said, shaking my head. "If you're done, I have to call an asshole."

"But you haven't yet," she pointed out.

"So?"

"So, being single is better than being in the wrong relationship."

The Demon had clearly had some therapy in her five hundred years.

"Got it. Thank you. Leave," I told her.

"Slash Gordon is nothing to you," she said. Again, ignoring my request to leave. "Relationships are like farts. If you have to force it, it's shit. That orgy-loving douche is a large, stinky turd. Never bang a piece of fecal matter."

I seriously hoped she wasn't being literal and speaking from experience.

Ophelia was on a roll. "First—the next time you want to fall in love, make sure that you're the crazy one, not him. Second—let the dude wear the pants, but make sure you tell him which ones to wear. Only gay men have good taste in clothing. And third—relationships are like the final-sale rack at Nordstrom. From a distance all that last-season crap looks amazing, but when you get up close, you realize that you'll be a fucking loser if you wear shit that's not in. Slash the Rash is so last season. Actually, I'm not sure he was ever in season."

I knew what she was doing. It was hard to believe that Ophelia was helping me, but she was. Some of her metaphors were questionable, but that was to be expected. She was correct. Slash the Rash was so last season. He couldn't hurt me because I no longer cared. My past made me the woman I was right now. I wasn't close to being perfect, but I was doing fine.

Of course, I'd be better if I didn't know I was a Demon who had a short shelf life due to the fact that I held the balance of the Darkness in my hands. But shit happens. It was either rise up or die trying.

"I hated you when I met you," I said, walking over to the bed and sitting on the edge. "I thought you were a vapid brainless idiot with big tits."

"Compliments will get you far," she quipped sarcastically.

"Not finished," I said with a grin. "I was wrong."

Her eyes widened and she blushed. It was sweet and sad. She covered it quickly. It was clear that flattery wasn't handed out to her often.

"Whatever," she said dismissively. "Point is, don't second guess your gut. It's obvious that you have the hots for Abaddon. Granted, he's insane, but he's a far better choice than a dude with a mullet. Just shove the past where it belongs and call the fucker for the passes."

I laughed. "I will. And you're right. Abaddon is a better bet than a mullet. Pretty sure I'll mess that one up too, but we have to save him first before I can screw up another relationship." I paused and gently cupped her cheek. "Thank you, Ophelia. For a Demon, you're a great gal."

"Do not let that shit get around," she said, pushing my hand away. "I pride myself on my bitchy rep."

I crossed my heart. "Your secret is safe with me, jackass."

She grinned. "Much better, bitch." She rolled off the bed and stood up. "Get to work, Demon. Time waits for no one."

And on those words, Ophelia left the room.

Wisdom came from the oddest places lately. Candy Vargo's advice was coming true—strange possibilities were definitely the way to go.

And they just kept on coming.

"Slash, it's Cecily. How are you?"

The silence on the other end of the line wasn't encouraging. It was mortifying.

"Cecily Bloom," I clarified. It was kind of presumptuous to think he remembered me. It had been decades since we'd last spoken. While my name wasn't all that common, it didn't mean he didn't know a ton of women named Cecily.

Still silence.

Shit.

"Cecily Bloom. We used to be married," I added lamely.

All the confidence Ophelia had given me flew right out of the window.

"Babe! Baby babe," Slash finally said. "Your sexy voice gave me a woody. My dick is standing at attention. So good to hear from you. Wazzzz up?"

I winced and gagged silently. "Not much." Polite conversation before the big ask seemed to be the way to go, but if he talked about his dick again, I was going in for the kill. "Has life been treating you well?"

"It'd be a lot better if you were bouncing on my rod," he said in a husky whisper.

This time I did gag. I covered it with a cough. Nice. I had to be nice. The conversation had the potential to end me faster than the flaming Demon assholes. "Such the joker," I said lightly, trying to move the chat away from his *rod*.

"Not joking, babe," he said. "You were it for me. I write all my songs for you, babe. You're the one who got away. 'My Love Stick' is all about you."

"Wow." That was way too much nightmare-inducing information. It was time for the ask. The exchange was making me want to call him a delusional, oversexed asshole. "Anyhoo, I was wondering—"

"I was wondering too," he said, cutting me off. "We were so good together. What happened to us, babe?"

"I think it was the orgy," I reminded him.

"Which one?" he asked, confused.

I blew out an audible breath and soldiered on. There was no way I was going to verbally relive the time I'd gone out to grab bagels and coffee for us and came back to the hotel room to find him getting it on with six busty women. I'd poured the hot coffee on his junk and threw the bagels at his *friends*. He'd wanted to sue for the third-degree burn on his balls, but the optics weren't good for him. He'd decided having the world know he'd had skin grafts on his nuts wasn't sexy. Slash Gordon was all about the sexy image. In the end, we'd gotten a quickie divorce. The son of a bitch had tried to get alimony, but Man-mom and Sean had made him sign an ironclad prenup. I had a great family.

Forcing myself to stay on track, I got back to the point of the call. "I'm in Vegas and heard you're playing the Golden Showers tonight."

"Got that right, babe," he said. "You wanna fuck before the show?"

Swallowing back my bile was hard. "Umm… no. But I'd like to come to the show. Do you have any backstage passes available?"

"Pretty sure I just blew my wad," he said, panting.

I was going to need a shower after the repulsive phone call.

"Congrats." I kept my tone pleasant. I was an actress. I leaned hard into my training. Honestly, I deserved an Oscar for not losing my shit. "Can I get thirty passes for tonight?"

"Holy fuck, babe," he said with a laugh. "You into orgies now?"

I closed my eyes and bit down on my lips so I didn't scream. "Sure," I lied.

"All thirty passes are for hot chicks like you?" he asked with a lewd laugh.

How in the hell had I thought I loved this man? He was disgusting.

"Gorgeous women," I told him. "Can I get the passes?"

"Can we have dinner back in LA next week?" he bargained.

Yelling 'Are you fucking kidding me?' wasn't the best plan. It was so close to flying from my lips, I slapped my free hand over my mouth. "Next week might be hard," I mumbled through splayed fingers. I immediately regretted my word choice.

"Can't be any harder than my cock right now," he said silkily. "Say yes, babe. I'll get you thirty passes if you have dinner with me next week. Tell you what… we'll even skip the orgy tonight. Well, unless you want to do it. Not sure I can bang thirty women, but I could give it the old Slash Gordon try."

"No," I shouted. "No orgy."

"And dinner, babe?" he pressed.

"Umm… sure," I said, caving in. Hell, I'd probably be dead and wouldn't have to go.

"Yessssss," he crowed. "Dinner with Shirley!"

I pressed my lips together so I didn't laugh. "It's Cecily."

"That's what I said, babe."

Gathering up all the pretending I had left in me, I plastered a smile on my face so my voice sounded normal. "Where should I pick up the passes?"

"Stage door, babe," Slash replied. "I'll have someone meet you at seven. Sound good?"

"Six forty-five would be better." I was meeting Lilith in the parking lot at seven. I didn't want to be late.

"Excited to see me, babe?" he purred.

"You have no idea," I replied.

"Got another boner popping up," Slash informed me. "Six forty-five it is. I'll see you after the show."

"Thank you, Slash." He was gross, but I had manners and I was going to use them. My dad had raised me right.

"Anytime, babe. Anytime."

I hung up, took off my Versace dress and jumped into the shower.

Washing the conversation off of me was going to take a while. It was a good thing it was nine AM. I had all day.

CHAPTER EIGHT

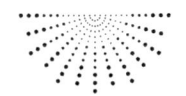

I was ready to rumble... I hoped.

After an hour and a half shower, I'd spent the rest of the day pacing the Presidential Suite in my Versace dress and heels. My stress level was high. Cher and Ophelia stayed quiet and out of my way. I'd texted Lilith that I would secure the passes. She'd sent back a heart emoji. I rolled my eyes and kept pacing.

And now we were on our way to the Golden Showers Bet and Bed.

I felt short of breath. The thought of Abaddon being tortured or worse made my skin crawl. He was weak because he'd sacrificed for me. Guilt raged inside me. Tonight, he would be free. I just hoped he was still alive. Surely, Lilith would have sent me a crying emoji or something stupider if anything had happened to him. My mother's unmerited and way-too-late concern for my safety would have made her tell me so I would stay away.

Putting my hand over my racing heart, I closed my eyes and pictured the man I would love to love if I got the chance. I mentally walked myself through the first time I'd seen him. Hostile would be an understated way to describe it.

I grinned as I thought about our meet-cute that wasn't remotely cute. Although Abaddon, even at his worst, made me smile. Clearly, I was nuts... and I didn't care.

That day had been bad and I was only hours away from getting fired from *Family Spies* for not having a big enough butt. He'd stood with the producers and glared at me. All six foot something of the man with hair as dark as mine and gorgeous blue eyes narrowed to slits stared furiously at me. It was unnerving and rude, but that didn't mean I didn't notice his lips were positively ridiculous and his body was lean and muscular under his expensive suit.

I'd thought he was insane when he told me I was a Demon. I'd nicknamed him Dick due to his personality. He'd hated it, which delighted me. But being a kind gal, even to an asshole, I'd recommended therapy. Of course, all that turned out to be moot when he'd proved his claim. I was sure he'd drugged me when he took me into the Darkness to show me my heritage.

He hadn't.

As frightening as the Darkness was, I'd felt an intense pull to the vast mountainous landscape of raging fire. The words wicked and sultry had come to mind as I'd watched the flames lick up the sides of trees bearing fruit I'd never seen. Swarms of brightly colored birds soared through the fire. Their wing spans were the size of a car and the sounds they made had reminded me of metal on metal in a deadly pileup of cars. My breath had come in quick spurts and I'd felt a strange kinship to the shocking scene. A huge red sun hung low in an inky purple sky.

It was horrifyingly gorgeous.

What did I expect? It was a version of Hell.

"Is my hair good?" Ophelia asked, jerking me back into reality.

She was good at that. "Yes. You're beautiful."

She grinned. "I know. Right?"

I rolled my eyes. "You're also extremely humble."

She looked appalled. "Is that a joke?" she demanded.

"Yes."

"Got worried there for a sec," she muttered, adjusting her girls.

A heavy silence ensued.

The drive to the casino seemed to take forever, yet at the same time it only took a moment. I was about to do as Lilith had asked. I'd get the passes. They'd be in my hands shortly and then in hers. I wasn't going to follow the rest of the orders.

I couldn't. It was wrong. It might be stupid, but I was going with my gut like Candy Vargo and Ophelia had told me to do. I leaned back in the leather seat and worked on breathing evenly. Sushi had insisted we use her Mercedes and driver. My pickup would look out of place. Apparently, Demons drove swanky cars.

A Succubus named Fifi was our driver. She was gorgeous and incredibly intimidating—about six feet tall, auburn hair, piercing green eyes and a resting bitch face that beat all I'd ever seen. Underneath her black Armani suit she was armed to the teeth. The woman had knives, guns and grenades. Fifi had shown us with little fanfare and great pride. When I'd asked why she had grenades, she'd grunted something unintelligible. Even Cher and Ophelia were surprised at the amount of hardware Fifi carried.

Sushi had stayed at her club. There was some kind of Immortal royalty showing up this evening. It was all kinds of hush-hush. Honestly, I didn't want to hear about it. Something told me the less I knew about the inner workings of the crazy, the better off I'd be.

Tonight, there was no script. There was no director. The set would be unfamiliar and my costume was advertising side boob. There was no rehearsal. It was an actor's nightmare. I was about to go onstage basically naked and not knowing my lines or blocking.

"I feel broken," I whispered.

"You're not broken, just bent," Ophelia assured me. "We're all a little nuts."

It was a better way of looking at life, but I struggled to get on board. The reality of dying sucked. A tingle shot through me and my stomach lurched. In a moment of total clarity, I realized I wanted to live. It was selfish. I was risking a lot of lives to want to see tomorrow. For all I knew, my death wouldn't even save Man-mom and Sean. If my identity was blown, it would stand to reason that Pandora would figure out that Lilith had loved—or possibly still loved—my dad. That would be enough for her to destroy him. That was for sure. If I was alive, I could protect him.

There were so many unanswered questions in my mind. I didn't know who to go to for answers. Candy Vargo seemed like a good bet, but I didn't know where she lived. Uncle Grim Reaper and his partner, Daisy, the Angel of Mercy, might be able to shed some light. But again, I had no clue where they lived or how to reach them.

"What's the plan?" Cher asked.

I glanced over at her. She had more red lipstick on her teeth than on her lips. It looked like she was bleeding. I smiled. Some things would never change. She was beautiful to me.

"Wipe your teeth," I told her, reaching into my bag and handing her a tissue. My fingers grazed a small box in the bag.

I giggled. The toothpicks I'd taken from Candy Vargo were with me. Using them in public was a no-go, but they gave me a calming sense of courage. "The plan is for me to pick up the passes at the stage door then deliver them to my mother at seven in the parking lot."

"Do we get to see the concert?" Ophelia asked.

I shook my head. "No."

"That sucks," she complained. "As repulsive as Slash the Rash is, he's pretty hot from a distance."

"He's over forty now," I reminded her. "And repulsive is an understatement. He's revolting." If the conversation from earlier was any indication, he'd gotten more disgusting with age.

"And you have to go to dinner with him next week," Ophelia said with a gag.

"Only if I'm alive," I muttered.

Fifi growled. It was terrifying. "Did this Slash the Rash person threaten your life, Cecily Bloom?"

Oh shit. "No," I said quickly. "I was joking."

The Succubus growled again. "Shall I bang him for you?" she inquired. "I can suck the life force out of him before his dick comes near my vagina."

I swallowed a very inappropriate laugh. "Umm... thank you, but no. I thought all of the Succubi were working on abstinence."

Fifi shrugged. "There are always exceptions to be made. I'm a big fan of *Camp Bite*. I often binge the reruns when I'm feeling murderous. Many lives have been saved due to the fictional undead antics of you and your brother. I have studiously avoided your brother Sean in his lifetime. I find him sexually attractive. However, I have too much admiration for his skill as an actor to bang him to death."

I was speechless… and horrified and grateful.

"Good on you," Cher said, patting Fifi's back. "I like a nutjob with restraint."

Fifi nodded curtly and pulled into the parking lot of the Golden Showers Bet and Bed. "We're here."

The casino was old and falling down on the outside. I was sure that was intentional. If I'd spotted it driving by, I would have kept on driving. All of the expensive cars parked outside might have given me pause, but not enough to check it out.

It was a large venue—definitely big enough for a rock concert. A menace floated in the air and I would swear a faint glittery gray mist swirled around the building. My chest tightened and I felt a tiny bit like I was levitating above my body.

"Bad vibes," Ophelia said with a shudder.

I couldn't have agreed more. So many thoughts and feelings raced inside me. Seeing my mother would be confusing. It wasn't a reunion. It was a transaction. The goal was Abaddon. Period. Everything I had to do centered on him. I pictured his beautiful face. I barely knew him, but it felt like I'd always known him. Maybe I was projecting, but figuring out what I was feeling wasn't on the agenda. That would come later… if there was a later.

Glancing down at my phone, my lips compressed into a thin line. We had five minutes before I picked up the passes. Scanning the parking lot, I looked for Lilith. The lot was empty of people and loaded with Jags, Mercedes and Rolls Royces. Sushi had been correct about my pickup standing out like a sore thumb.

"Need to find the stage door," I said, taking a deep and calming breath.

Improv wasn't my thing, but I was about to make it my thing.

Fifi started the car again and drove us to the back left side of the ramshackle building. "Right there," she grunted, reaching into her jacket and offering me a grenade.

I stared at it. "Not sure I need that."

"Everyone needs a grenade," Fifi insisted. "Gets the job done fast."

I nodded politely and still didn't take it. "I'm just picking up passes. Not nuking people."

"Take it," she demanded in a tone that almost made me pee my pants. Fifi was as terrifying as the flaming asshole Demons who had tried to end me. I was thankful she was on my team. "If you need it, pull the pin and throw it fast. If you don't end up using it, you can return it to me."

Cher elbowed me.

Swallowing my hesitation, I took the grenade. Putting it into my purse, I prayed to things I didn't believe in that I wouldn't find it necessary to pull the pin.

"Thank you," I choked out. "I'm sure I'll be returning it to you shortly."

"Being sure before you know what you're dealing with leads to death," Fifi stated emotionlessly. "Be flexible, Cecily Bloom. Be ready. If something comes at you, eliminate first, ask questions after."

I didn't want to point out that it was fruitless to ask questions of the dead. Pissing Fifi off seemed like a bad plan. Even Cher and Ophelia were silent. Candy Vargo's warning was at the forefront of my brain... *Stay true, follow your gut and trust your power. Remember that people with more experience tend to make better decisions than people who don't, and being a martyr is bullshit.*

Clearly, Fifi had more experience than me. Using a grenade wasn't my first choice. Ever. That being said, I wasn't going to forget I had it. I'd use it as a very last resort. Pulling up my purple fire sword and lopping off the bad guys' heads was preferable to blowing up a casino that had innocent humans like Slash the Rash Gordon in it.

"Wait," I said. "Is Slash human?"

"One hundred percent," Ophelia confirmed. "And an incredibly stupid one."

"Word," Cher agreed. "Let's get this party started!"

We did.

We got the party started with a bang… a big bang.

CHAPTER NINE

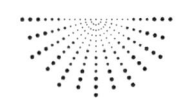

GETTING THE PASSES WAS EASY. THE NOTE FROM SLASH describing my privates in great detail was offensive and stomach churning. I'd handed it back to the mullet-sporting gentleman—for lack of a better term—who'd met me at the door.

All of that was expected.

The flaming asshole Demons with him were not. As soon as they spotted me, they lit up like Christmas trees on crack.

That was bad.

They quickly exited the building and slammed the door shut behind them. This had not been part of the plan.

"Run," I shouted at Ophelia and Cher. "Get them away from the building."

My only thoughts were for Abaddon's safety. If I screwed it all up before we got in, he was toast. My gut told me the best way to go was to eliminate the enemy as far from the casino as possible. I was going with my gut. It was all I had right now.

Ophelia poofed into an overgrown grassy area about two football fields away. Cher's wings exploded from her back and she flew. I was in trouble. I had to run. Yes, I jogged, but I'd never jogged for my life. I supposed there was a first time for everything.

Abaddon was going to be so pissed at me if I died after he'd done so much to keep me alive.

I felt a freezing-cold wind at my back. The flaming assholes emitted heat. I didn't have time to see what else was chasing me. Of course, when she scooped me up into her arms and ran so fast I was sure I was going to faint, I caught a glimpse.

It was Fifi. Fifi was pissed. She was also terrifying.

"Throw the grenade," she grunted. "It will buy time."

"On it," I said, reaching into my bag and pulling it out. "Will it kill them?"

"Sadly, no. We're going to have to do that ourselves. THROW IT!"

With shaking hands, I pulled the pin and lobbed it over Fifi's shoulder. The shocked screams were good. Fifi's crazed laugh sent chills up my spine. Whatever. It wasn't like we were going to hang out in real life.

She dropped me to the ground when we caught up with Cher and Ophelia. Cher was topless and wielding some kind of glowing golden stick. It looked like a massive dildo. I almost laughed.

Ophelia had her purple fire sword and no longer looked like a bimbo. The Demon was as badass as she'd advertised.

Fifi was shocking. She morphed into some kind of hulking, six-foot monster with razor-sharp fangs.

I wished I was dreaming. It was a lot to take in. Unfortunately, I wasn't. The hot shitshow was my life and potentially my death.

The flaming Demon assholes arrived only seconds behind Fifi and me. The grenade had done very little harm to them.

They looked the same as the others who'd tried to kill me in LA. This time, like the last, I had no plans to die.

There were five of them and four of us. The disgusting men with Goat Eyes were literally on fire—green fire with icy-blue sparks flying off their enormous bodies. The searing heat that arrived with the five assholes made me feel lightheaded and sick to my stomach. The putrid smell of sulfur wafted in the air.

"Excellent. Who knew it would be this easy? The spawn who can destroy all shall be decapitated." The man's voice sounded like he'd swallowed broken glass.

His cohorts laughed.

"Not today," I ground out.

"What the hell is he talking about?" Ophelia demanded.

The enemy shot her an amused glance. "You don't know who she is?"

"She's Cecily Bloom, motherfucker," Ophelia hissed. "Star of *Camp Bite*. AND SHE CAN FLY."

"That's right, you ugly bastards," Cher bellowed, waving her dildo in the air. "And I rep her, which gives me more pleasure than an orgasm."

"Seriously?" Fifi asked.

"Completely," Cher assured the monster version of the Succubus.

I winced. This wasn't going well. The truth needed to come from me. Not the assholes. The truth would hopefully set me free...

"I'm Lilith's daughter," I said, keeping my eyes on the deadly Demons.

"You. Are. Shitting. Me," Ophelia screeched.

"Don't I wish," I muttered. I hoped with all my might she wasn't about to switch teams. That would suck ass.

"I'm going to get so many brownie points for saving you," she crowed.

One wish granted.

"Kill them all," the flaming asshole grunted. "We shall bring the head of the abomination to the Goddess Pandora."

"In your dreams," Fifi screeched. "I'll bang all of you until you're six fucking feet under."

"Not sure we have time for that," I told her as they advanced.

"You're right. My bad," she said, pulling out her weapons.

They went for Cher, Ophelia and Fifi. It was as if I didn't exist.

That was a huge mistake on their part.

The fire that covered their bodies sparked and grew hotter. I felt rooted to the ground. Sweat poured down my face. Where was my purple fire sword? I watched in horror as they ripped Cher's wings from her body and then went for Ophelia like a runaway freight train straight from the bowels of Hell. Fifi was throwing grenades and daggers.

Nothing worked.

The tingling started in my toes and quickly spread through my body. No one was going to harm the people I cared about. I was so over this shit.

The sparks of fire that shot from my fingertips felt glorious. The flames licked up my arms and consumed me. The Demons were too stupid to notice.

Their second mistake.

The ringing in my ears was loud, but there was a rhythm to it. The drum beat was sensual and animalistic. I went with it. My purple fire sword appeared in my right hand. But to my great and grateful surprise, another materialized in my left.

I laughed. It was unhinged, but so was I. The power was

intoxicating. My entire body shook with a rage so intense, I hoped I wasn't about to lose control and kill everyone here. Uncle freaking Grim Reaper better have been true to his word. He'd promised he'd given me the tools to control my magic. It was time to test it out.

Granted, I felt completely out of control, but I was banking that my aim would be accurate. I saw the enemy through a bloody red mist. My friends were bathed in a golden light. Perfect.

Go for the red. Ignore the gold.

"You want me? Come and get me," I bellowed.

The imbeciles didn't listen. They didn't even glance over.

Third mistake. Three's a charm... for me. Some might say it's a crowd. Others might call it company. I called it kismet.

Slashing my swords in a downward motion, I screamed. I was fully on fire and explosions detonated with each move I made. My goal was red.

Ophelia, Cher and Fifi were open-mouthed and gobsmacked. I decided to take that as a good sign.

I shuddered. It felt like I left my body and floated above myself. I watched dispassionately as I moved through the crackling fires I'd created with speed that belonged to someone else. Without much thought or any remorse, I beheaded each flaming asshole. It was fast. It was precise. It was violent. It was done.

I turned and vomited as they lay in smoldering piles.

When I'd finished emptying my stomach, I walked over and stood by them as they dissolved into nothing. "Do not fuck with my people. It will not end well."

"Oh my freaking GOD," Cher shouted, limping over holding her wings in her hands. "That was genius!"

"You, Cecily Bloom, are a walking grenade," Fifi

announced, dropping to her knees before me. "I am at your service from this day forward. Forever. I will never leave your side."

That didn't sound all that good, but I wasn't going to make her feel bad. Having Fifi as a permanent fixture was a terrifying prospect.

"What the ever-loving fuck?" Ophelia gasped out, handing me a mint, which I gratefully accepted. "That was the badassiest thing I've ever seen."

She too dropped to her knees.

I felt the bile rise in my throat again as Pandora's henchmen turned to ash. I wiggled my fingers and created a wind. They blew away. "Good riddance to bad rubbish."

I glanced over at the casino. There was no one watching and no one else after me. My gut had been correct. We hadn't announced our presence.

The clapping behind me, however, threw me off. It wasn't Cher. It wasn't Ophelia. It wasn't Fifi. When the new addition spoke, I recognized the voice. It sent happy tingles through my body, which infuriated me.

Ophelia pressed her forehead to the ground and prostrated herself before her Goddess. Cher bowed her head in reverence. Only Fifi seemed unimpressed. The Succubus was the baddest of the badasses.

Slowly, I turned around.

My breath caught in my throat. It was all I could do not to cry. The woman standing ten feet away looked like me. There were definitely differences, but there was no denying we were related. There was a kindness in her eyes that cut me to the core. I'd wished for this moment all my life. It was here and it felt all wrong. This was not about me. It wasn't about us. There *was* no us.

"Lilith," I said flatly.

"Cecily," she replied, studying my face with great interest. "You're beautiful."

I shrugged and fought the urge to run to her. "Genetics. Beauty means very little. I have the passes." At least, I hoped I did. I'd shoved them into my purse before I ran to get the Demons away from the casino.

Thankfully, Fifi had my bag. "My liege," Fifi said, handing me the passes. She really was useful—spine-tinglingly scary but useful

"Thank you, Fifi," I said. I was grateful to the Succubus, but I was no one's liege and had no intention to be. "Call me Cecily, please."

"As you wish, my liege Cecily," she replied.

We needed to work on that.

Handing Lilith the backstage passes, I looked her in the eye. "I'm coming in with you. Abaddon is my responsibility. I'm going to fight for him."

My mother was alone. That surprised me. The fact that her lips compressed wasn't surprising. Not one bit.

"That's unwise," she said coolly.

"It's the way it is," I replied just as coldly.

She began to pace back and forth. Maybe I'd gotten my pacing habit from her. She touched Ophelia's head and bent down to kiss her cheek.

It irked me that I was jealous.

"You've done well, Ophelia," she said.

"Thank you, my Goddess," she replied. "My loyalty is with you and your daughter, Cecily Bloom."

My mother nodded and moved on. "Joan of Arc," Lilith said as she approached my agent the Angel. "It's good to see you again."

Cher grinned and put her shirt back on. "Going by Cher now. Borrowing the name Joan of Arc was a damned disaster. Can't even tell you how many times I was almost burned at the stake."

"Cher fits you," Lilith said with a smile. "Are you well enough to heal everyone? I'll be indebted to you."

"You bet your Demon bippy and this one is on me," Cher said, waving her hand and healing herself first. "Get over here, Fifi. I think you might have shot your foot off."

"Actually, I lopped it off with a dagger by accident," Fifi told her as she morphed back into her redheaded, green-eyed form and limped over. "I shot myself in the head."

"Not to worry," Cher said with a chuckle. "I've got you."

This was not normal, but I was seriously thankful that my agent could repair us. Ophelia was bleeding from all her orifices and missing a hand. I looked down at myself and gasped. Other than my dress being torn and singed, I didn't have a scratch on me.

"Genetics," Lilith said, noticing my surprise. "You're very hard to kill, child."

I gave her a pointed and hard stare. "All the more reason for me to come with you."

Lilith stood silently for a long moment then snapped her fingers. I was no longer in a ripped Versace dress with an obscene amount of side boob exposed. I was sporting black cargo pants, a matching fitted long-sleeved t-shirt and black combat boots. My attire was perfect as concert stage crew. Lilith dressed herself similarly, along with Cher, Ophelia and Fifi.

Warm heat engulfed me as a glittering red mist danced around me. A chemical change occurred in my body. It was difficult to breathe, but I took it like a badass. I wasn't sure what Lilith was doing, but I trusted her enough to believe she wasn't going to kill me.

"Wowza," Cher said, giving me a thumbs up. "You're a knockout as a blonde."

"I'm not blonde," I said, a bit bewildered.

"You are now, my liege Cecily Bloom," Fifi assured me.

"It's a disguise," Lilith explained. "We look too much alike for Pandora not to notice. She's definitely aware of your existence. From what we've learned, she's expecting you. It's the reason she took Abaddon. Under orders from Pandora, Rhoda Spark had been waiting for an opening and took it when she saw it. She will be punished severely. I'm quite sure Pandora has seen your picture. We won't make it easy for her."

"So, I'm coming with you?" I asked, touching my new blonde tresses.

Lilith raised a brow. "I didn't think I had a choice."

"You don't," I said quickly.

"As you wish, Cecily," she said. "But beware of what you wish for."

I let her words settle. Living with myself would be impossible if I didn't try. According to my lovely and very dead Uncle Joe, the only way to fail is not to try.

"I have one question," I said.

"Just one?" my mother asked.

I nodded. "Will Abaddon recognize me like this?"

"If what both Pandora and I suspect is true, Abaddon will recognize you in any form you take until the end of time. It will be interesting to test the theory."

Her words relieved and confused me. Her tone was loaded, but I ignored it. I would dissect the meaning later.

"Let's get this party started," I said, stealing Cher's line.

My mother smiled. It was filled with love and pride. I

pushed down the anger that welled up inside me and simply accepted it at face value. It was better for her to be proud than pissed. I knew what I could do when pissed. I couldn't begin to imagine what Lilith could do.

"Yes," she said, extending her hand to me. "Let's get this party started."

I took it and walked back to the casino. My hand felt right in hers. I hated it as much as I loved it.

Cher had been quick with her healing, and she, Ophelia and Fifi followed close behind us.

We were a fearsome fivesome, and we were going to kick some ass.

CHAPTER TEN

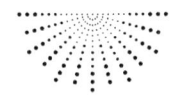

A GROUP OF DEMONS WHO WERE LOYAL TO LILITH WAITED FOR us in a deserted alcove at the back of the building—both male and female. The age range looked to be between twenty-five and mid-forties. Looks could be very deceiving. I was sure most were older than dirt. Lilith wouldn't bring inexperienced Demons. I was the only one with that liability.

They were absurdly attractive and all of them stared at me with unabashed curiosity. The Demons were wary of my presence. A good majority appeared downright hostile. It reminded me of Abaddon on our first meeting. They clearly knew who I was. I didn't blame them for being on guard. I was the newly discovered piece of a deadly and horrifying puzzle and a danger to everyone here according to the prophecy.

Not my fault. If they had a problem with me, they could take it up with their Goddess. I didn't ask to be born.

"Not much security around this place," I commented, looking around.

"This is Pandora's territory. She feels no need for security," a male Demon said, bowing his head to Lilith and me. "Her arrogance is astounding. It shall be her undoing. I'm Dagon."

Thankfully, there was one friendly face. I held out my hand. "I'm Cecily."

Dagon looked wildly confused and took my hand with great caution. He glanced over at Lilith. She nodded. "It is an honor to be in your presence, Goddess Cecily."

I forced a smile. It seemed as if I'd broken some kind of protocol with the handshake. Whatever. I didn't know the damn rules. What I did know was that I didn't want to be called Goddess or liege. My profession was acting. I was perfectly fine with Cecily. "Nice to meet you too, Dagon."

Lilith gave the passes to Ophelia and directed her to hand them out. I slipped mine over my head and watched as each Demon came forward to take their pass. Cher and Fifi stood behind me to my left. Ophelia was behind me to my right. Lilith stood by my side. One by one the Demons stepped forward. Each bowed to Lilith and me before approaching Ophelia.

It was unsettling and strange. I was no better than any of these people. Royalty—for lack of a more fitting term—was absurd.

Lilith stepped away to speak with Dagon. He was obviously her second-in-command. The bowing made me uncomfortable. I tried to think of it as an acting role, but it didn't work. This wasn't pretend. It was real. I stepped back and stood next to Ophelia. The shocked gasps from the Demons were loud. Ophelia grinned like a fool.

I'd probably broken another rule, but at this point I didn't care. I'd just lopped five heads off and puked my guts up. Breaking the rules was nothing.

"You okay, bitch?" Ophelia asked quietly.

I'd never thought of the word bitch as a term of endearment until now. My lip quirked. "Fine, jackass."

A stunning woman with eyes narrowed to glittering slits approached for a pass. She glared at me. I came very close to rolling my eyes. It was tough, but I held back. It was probably bad form to get into a fight with someone on the same team. While my mother's opinion of me didn't matter, I didn't want her to be disappointed.

Who was I kidding? Her opinion mattered to me as much as I didn't want to cop to it.

I kept my expression blank as the nasty woman continued to shoot daggers from her eyes my way. Were all Demons assholes? The answer was looking like a resounding yes.

"Give me my pass," she snapped at Ophelia.

My buddy wasn't having it. She dangled the pass just out of the woman's reach. "What's the magic word, Shiva?"

"Give. Me. My. Pass," she snarled.

She was talking to Ophelia, but her gaze stayed on me.

I smiled. It didn't reach my eyes. She looked like she was about to lose her shit. "I believe you were asked to use the magic word," I said in a flat tone.

She opened her mouth to speak several times, but nothing came out. It was crystal clear that she wanted to end me. If she was my ally, I was screwed.

Shiva's face turned an unattractive blood red and her fists clenched at her sides. Her face screwed up into an expression that made her heinous. When she spoke, it was as ugly as she'd become. "You are the reason the Goddess is here," she hissed. "If anything happens to my Goddess, I'll kill you."

My heart plummeted with fear, but I schooled my expression to stay neutral. "Noted," I replied icily. They seemed to respect power and bad behavior. Fine. I could play that game.

I took the pass from Ophelia's hand and put it over Shiva's head. As she tried to back away, I held onto the cord and pulled her close. The crowd went silent and watched with rabid interest. I didn't care. If I got offed by one of my mother's minions, she would be furious.

I went nose to nose with the awful Demon. "You do not have to like me. I do not have to like you, and trust me, I don't. You're a nasty piece of work. Lilith's safety is as concerning to me as Abaddon's. I just decapitated five flaming assholes so our approach wouldn't be detected. Your shitty attitude is pissing me off. It's a real bad plan to piss me off."

"She dusted them all by herself," Ophelia added, bursting with pride. "Never seen shit like that in all my years. Cecily has TWO purple fire swords."

The Demons gasped and whispered amongst themselves. I ignored it. However, I held up my hand to my over-sharing, well-intentioned buddy. She zipped it.

Turning my attention back to Shiva, I winked at her. She blanched. "If you mess with me, it will be the last thing you do, Sheba."

"It's Shiva," she said as fear sparked in her eyes.

I shrugged. "Whatever. Have I made myself clear?"

"You have," she ground out through clenched teeth.

"What's the magic word for my friend Ophelia?" I demanded.

"Please," she hissed like a snake.

"Awesome," I said. "Shall we hug it out?"

She wanted to deck me… or worse. I knew I was pushing it, but she was chapping my ass. Looking over my shoulder for the bad guys who wanted to kill me was getting old. I certainly didn't want to look over my shoulder for the good guys trying to kill me—good being a relative word.

Shiva jerked away and disappeared into the crowd. The formerly hostile Demons were now far less hostile. I closed my eyes. This was ridiculous. I felt bad about how ugly I'd been to Shiva, but I had no time to be challenged by a Demon who was supposed to be on my team. As bad as I felt about lowering myself to her level, I had to admit the acceptance of the others was a relief. I hoped I wouldn't have to do many repeat performances of mean Cecily. Mean wasn't my modus operandi.

Ophelia leaned in. "Everyone hates Shiva," she whispered. "But it's kind of a given why she would want a go at you."

I was confused. "What did I do to her?"

"Nothing," she assured me. "It's Abaddon. She banged him on and off for a few centuries. She fell and he didn't. She has a hard-on for anyone he cares about."

I wrinkled my nose. That was too much information. The news icked me out and made my little green monster roar just below the surface. Jealousy sucked. Normally, jealousy wasn't in my repertoire. Today, it was. I didn't own Abaddon any more than he owned me. We hadn't even gone on a date yet. What was the matter with me? Chances were that any attempt at a relationship would blow up in my face like all my others.

Of course, I did have a few questions that made me want to puke again... "Are they still banging?"

"Hell no," she told me with a laugh. "Abaddon called that disaster off two hundred years ago after he found out she was trying to get pregnant to trap him."

"Apparently she didn't get the memo," I said.

"True that," she agreed then handed out the rest of the passes.

Lilith was still talking with Dagon. I hoped she hadn't witnessed the little showdown, but I was pretty sure she didn't miss much. I almost screamed when Fifi snuck up behind me and whispered in my ear. I hadn't heard or seen her move. The Succubus was either really stealthy or I needed to pay more attention to my surroundings.

"I don't usually bang women, but for you, my liege, I would be happy to screw the life out of the one who tried to challenge you," she offered.

I inhaled deeply. Fifi was going to be a problem if she kept offering to screw all my enemies to death. "Umm... that's very, you know, loyal, Fifi. But I'm going to have to take a pass. I can handle Shiva."

"As you wish," she replied and moved away as quietly as she'd arrived.

Cher was yucking it up with a few Demons and trying to get them to sign contracts with her. I shook my head. My agent was always working.

"We shall move in small groups," Lilith announced, walking back over. "There are six entrances. Five to an entrance and space it out."

Cher raised her hand. Lilith acknowledged her.

"Do we have a plan?" Cher inquired.

Lilith looked at her people and smiled. "We do not. We're winging it."

"Shit," Cher muttered.

"Not to worry," my mother assured her. "We're not completely winging it. I'll be in communication with all of you when we're inside. The primary goal is Abaddon. He may or may not be at full power. We will proceed as if he's not. Secondary goal is Rhoda."

The Demons growled. Lilith's expression turned hard. Her dark hair began to blow around her head and a shimmering red mist surrounded her. She looked like the Angel of Death—glorious and terrifying. Goose bumps popped up on my arms

THE EDGE OF EVIL

and I was reminded this was not a joke. It was real and potentially deadly. I wasn't sure how she was going to communicate with us, but I didn't say a word. They obviously had a system.

Lilith went on in a tone that I would hate to be on the other end of. "Rhoda has betrayed me. I want her taken alive if possible. If necessary, end her. I do not accept betrayal lightly."

"Your style is vicious," Fifi said, displaying her arsenal to the group. They were impressed. "I admire violence."

"Thank you," Lilith replied.

With a wave of her hand, Lilith gifted everyone with a disguise. Everyone was still stunning, but muted somehow—less noticeable.

"Fifi, Cher, Ophelia, Dagon and Shiva will protect Cecily," Lilith commanded. "I'll move between groups. Everyone, go. Now."

I bit down on my lip so I didn't say something awful. Having the former lover of Abaddon protecting me was not a good plan.

As everyone dispersed silently, I pulled Lilith aside. I was aware our small team could hear me. I didn't care. My safety was perilous to begin with. Having to watch Shiva while I watched my own ass wasn't working for me. "I don't want Shiva on my team."

Lilith raised a brow. "Shiva will fight harder for Abaddon's safety than anyone here."

"With all due respect, you're wrong," I said evenly. "I'll hold that title. I don't trust Shiva."

"However, I do," Lilith replied. "The words you exchanged with her were just words. Respect is earned. Earn it."

"Can't do that if I'm dead," I shot back. I reached into my bag and pulled out the box of toothpicks I'd taken from Candy Vargo. They tingled with magic in my hand. Placing two in my mouth, I dropped my bag to the ground and stared at my mother. "Want one?"

Her brows shot up high. "Where did you get those?"

"From a friend."

She shook her head and sighed. "Candy Vargo?"

"Yes."

Lilith tilted her head and eyed me. "*Candy Vargo* is your friend?"

"Absolutely." Now, she wasn't exactly a long-time buddy and hanging out with her seemed beyond iffy, but she'd been honest and had my best interests in mind. That was big in my book.

Dagon and Shiva gasped. Both appeared shocked, alarmed and terrified. Candy Vargo's reputation was clearly known far and wide. I wasn't sure what they knew. My guess was that it was her one-time go around with cannibalism. It was still difficult to wrap my mind around that. However, I judged people on how they treated me. She had treated me well.

"She gave them to me," I replied. "Told me to go with my gut and trust my power."

Lilith took two toothpicks and put them in her mouth. "Was that all she said?"

"Nope. She also said, 'Remember that people with more experience tend to make better decisions than people who don't, and being a martyr is bullshit.'"

"And that was the most important part," she said, then pulled a ruby-encrusted dagger from her pocket and sliced the palm of her hand. She offered me the bloody dagger. "Do the same, Cecily."

My mouth had formed a perfect O. The cut was deep and she was seriously bleeding. "Is it going to hurt?" I asked. I was used to special effects and stunt doubles, not the real thing.

"A lot less than dying," she replied dryly.

Lilith had made her point. I took the dagger. It felt heavy and vibrated in my hand. The enchantment was obvious. The plot of this episode had taken a turn into Crazy Town. Sucking in a quick breath, I went for it. The razor-sharp dagger sliced my hand like a hot knife through frozen butter. My blood spurted. I stared as it dripped down my fingertips and onto the gravel by my feet. The sensation was searingly painful, but I sucked it up and refused to wince.

Lilith clasped her hand in mine. Her gaze was focused, intense and somewhat frightening. She stood as still as a statue—a beautiful, terrifying Goddess made of stone. For a hot sec, I thought I was going to pass out from blood loss. Of course, because life was batshit nuts, we ignited. Our joined hands caught fire. It was as black as the Darkness. I watched in fascination as the flames moved up our arms in a circular motion. It was a mini tornado of fire. The most shocking part was that it didn't hurt—at all. The rush was quick and all-consuming, followed by a sense of absolute calm.

It ended so quickly I felt a bizarre sense of sorrow. Lilith removed her hand from mine and smiled.

"Will this give me new tricks?" I asked, examining my palm as it healed before my eyes.

"Think of it as a boost," she said with a wink then left me behind as she walked toward the stage door. "Best when used for others."

My life was out of control.

The Immortals were cryptic, but this time I'd understood what she'd meant about Candy's words of wisdom. Shiva had way more experience than me. Lilith had come to this plane because I wouldn't back down. Apparently, she was in as much danger as Abaddon… and me. It was a good possibility that my mother wanted Shiva with her and it had nothing to do with me.

Fine. I would not be a martyr and I wouldn't be responsible for making anyone else a martyr either. If I could boost someone by becoming *blood-brothers or rather blood-sisters* with my mother, I would. Getting in Shiva's way wasn't going to happen. The goal was Abaddon's safety. My feelings of dislike didn't weigh in. If Lilith trusted her, I would take my lead from her.

However, I wasn't going to lay down and take anything that Shiva wanted to hand out.

Dagon, Cher, Ophelia, Fifi and Shiva stood ready and waiting for me to move.

"Shiva," I said, giving her a level stare. "Lilith trusts you. I choose to do the same."

She smiled and bared her teeth like an animal. It wasn't pretty.

"But," I added in a voice as cold as ice as my fingers lit up and fire engulfed my entire body. "If you mess with me or put Abaddon in danger because you despise me, I'll come at you and make the rest of your eternity a living hell. Dead or alive."

She was no longer smiling.

"And those are not idle words," I said, snapping my fingers and dousing the flames. I was surprised and wildly happy that I hadn't burned the clothes off my body. Old Uncle Grim Reaper was pretty good at his job. "The words are a promise. I don't break my promises."

She nodded her head. There was fear in her eyes. I despised playing mean Cecily, but what I liked or didn't like was irrelevant. Only Abaddon and Lilith's safety was important. I didn't want to die, but if that was what fate held in store then so be it. But I wasn't going to die by Shiva's hand.

"I don't care if the truce is just for tonight. Tomorrow, you can hate me again. Tonight, we're on the same side. Am I clear?"

"Crystal," she replied in a subdued tone. She bowed to me then extended her hand.

It was a bizarre peace offering that she was breaking etiquette.

I shook it. "The goal is keeping Abaddon and Lilith alive. Period. Everything else is fair game."

Shiva still held my hand in hers. "No martyrs," she reminded me with a look of respect in her eyes. It wasn't friendly, but it was a start.

I paused, then I smiled. It was a real smile. "Correct," I admitted. "No martyrs." Glancing around, I looked at my people—Cher, Ophelia, Fifi, Dagon and Shiva. Lilith stood in front of the closed stage door and watched. "Let's get this party started."

And we did.

CHAPTER ELEVEN

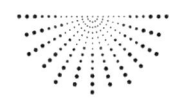

The backstage area was busy. Our presence wasn't noticed as odd. The passes were the key. While I didn't feel safe, I didn't feel like a red herring either.

My eyes were wide open and I stayed aware of my surroundings. I was pretty sure I was insane, but I would swear I felt Abaddon's presence. It was most likely wishful thinking, but I couldn't shake it.

Lilith had disguised herself before we entered. She was a faded version of her glorious self with strawberry-blonde hair instead of her dark curls, and she had a slighter build. As different as she looked, I recognized her at a bone-deep level. I wasn't sure what that meant, but it was a relief to realize that I could help watch over her no matter how much she changed her appearance.

The interior of the building was luxurious in an over-the-top way—even the backstage area. It wasn't like any concert venue I'd visited. Massive crystal chandeliers hung from the rafters and glittered in the roving spotlights. The floors were a highly sheened black marble. The uber-cool level was at an all-time high. I'd never seen so many absurdly attractive people in one place in my life—and I lived in Hollywood.

"Holy cow," Cher muttered, pulling an eye pencil out of her pocket and going to town on her lips. "Talk about some moolah."

I agreed and took the lime-green pencil away from her. Looking diseased wasn't good for staying under the radar. She didn't miss a beat. Cher pulled out a purple eye pencil and continued her routine. At least purple was better than green…

"Look busy," Dagon instructed.

We walked over to a table along the back wall and began folding t-shirts with an image of Slash Gordon front and center. I almost laughed. The man looked ridiculous. Slash's jewels were… large. It was false advertising. Unfortunately, I had proof. The idiot had put a salami in his pants or they'd photoshopped the crotch of his spandex leggings to a level that was laughable.

"Total douche," Ophelia muttered with a giggle.

"And then some," I agreed as I paid mind to my surroundings.

An unsettling feeling of menace hung in the air combined with a heavy sexual undertone. There was no band performing, but an undeniable primal beat was vibrating in the background. I felt myself being pulled in. My body reacted on a visceral level. I gripped the edge of the table like it was a lifeline and I was about to drown. Ophelia put her hand over mine and squeezed tight.

"Think about something gross," she whispered in my ear.

"What do you mean?"

"It's all an illusion—magic," she explained. "Pandora controls her people by manipulating desire. It's messed up. In a few hours this place will be a massive disgusting orgy."

I wanted to gag. "Help me. I feel strange—like I want to get naked and do stuff I'll seriously regret."

"Picture your dad's wrinkled balls," she suggested. "Or falling into an outhouse toilet full of shit and swallowing a gallon of turds. Or visualize Candy Vargo eating Angels."

That did it. I was so grossed out I was close to losing what little I had left in my stomach. Ophelia was now a lifelong friend.

"Thank you, jackass," I choked out.

"No worries, bitch," she replied with a grin.

I went back to folding shirts and studied the others roaming around. I wasn't sure who was human and who wasn't. No one was flaming like the assholes I'd recently beheaded.

"Dagon," I whispered. "Can you tell who is human?"

He nodded and continued to arrange the merchandise. "Have you ever blurred your eyes to look at Christmas tree lights?"

It was a little weird to think of a Demon celebrating Christmas, but that wasn't any of my business. I knew what he meant. "Yes."

"Immortals glow when you squint. Humans do not."

That was nifty news. I tried it out. I kind of wished I hadn't. Aside from about five people, we were surrounded by Demons.

"Thank you."

"My pleasure," he replied then eyed me very seriously. "A word to the wise. The blood of a Goddess is more powerful than magic."

I stared at him. I wasn't sure what to do with the information. "And?"

"And in knowing that, use it as only a Goddess can."

"Would you care to be more specific?" I asked, hearing the

panic in my voice. I was already a loose cannon. What I didn't need was more power I couldn't control. When Lilith had said it was a boost, I assumed it was an enhancement to what I already had. Never assume... makes an ass out of you and me. And possibly a dead ass.

He smiled. "I'm not a Goddess. Therefore, I can't answer the question."

"Shit," I muttered, looking around for Lilith. She was nowhere to be seen. "Shit, shit, shit."

"Standing still isn't prudent," Dagon said, assessing the situation. He moved us away from the table and into the hustle and bustle. "Act like you know where you're going and what you're doing."

I nodded. That I could do. I was playing a role. I'd pretended my entire life. Today I was a roadie on a concert tour. Snatching up a box of water bottles from a table, I handed them out as we passed people by. I might not know how to use my power, but I sure as hell knew how to act.

Ophelia had picked up some cables and walked right onto the stage. I watched as she began to plug them into the mics and instruments while scanning the crowd. I hoped she knew what she was doing and didn't end up electrocuting herself.

Fifi was on my heels and followed my every move. She was so quiet it was easy to forget she was there. Cher moved like a pro and proceeded to chat up the stage management. She was so knowledgeable that no one batted an eye. Shiva followed the crew who climbed into the rafters to run the lights. Dagon kept his hand lightly on my back and guided us toward the house. I didn't see Lilith anywhere.

That concerned me.

Before I could check in with Dagon, I ran smack into my ex-husband. Literally. The wind got knocked out of both of us.

Fifi steadied me and stayed by my side. Dagon moved a few feet away, but kept his eyes on the action. Shiva was in the rafters above holding a massive spotlight, ready to drop it on Slash if he caused a problem. I was pretty sure it would be a big problem if we offed the lead singer of the musical act…

While I was fairly sure I couldn't handle Pandora on my own, I knew I could handle my ex.

Or I thought I could…

Slash Gordon was surrounded by an entourage of mullet-sporting, spandex-wearing, middle-aged losers. Of course, the large-breasted, scantily clad groupies were along for the ride too. My ex shoved his redheaded, chesty gal pal to the side, much to her horror, and focused his attention on me. It was clear that the idiot had no clue who I was.

"Baby, baby, baaaabay," he purred, looking me up and down like I was a piece of meat. "You're so hot, my zipper's falling for you. I can tell you're an archaeologist. I have a *big* bone for you to examine. So, howsaboutit, sexy mama?"

Was he for real? Not only did I want to slap him for his sexist and obscene come-ons, I wanted to slap myself for ever thinking he was something special. I was open-mouthed, shocked and appalled. It was tempting to point out that his repulsive spandex pants didn't have a zipper, but the words wouldn't come out.

Fifi tensed up beside me like a bomb about to detonate. She covertly slipped a grenade and a knife into my pocket. This could get out of hand quickly. Ending Slash Gordon in a permanent way wasn't on the agenda. He was an asshole, but that wasn't a good enough reason to kill the jerk.

Unfortunately, Slash didn't get the memo and the imbecile took my silence as approval to keep going.

He tossed his long hair over his shoulder. The groupie gals

swooned and giggled. The rest of the entourage mimicked his moves. It was embarrassing.

"What's your name, sunshine?" he inquired then held up his hand. "Wait. Don't tell me. I think I'll call you Sunshine."

"Sunshine," the entourage murmured and applauded.

If I'd read this exchange on paper, I would have gotten gas—explosive gas.

"So Sunshine, I like to be on top of things. Would you like to be one of them?" Slash asked with a shit-eating grin. That got a big laugh from his sycophants. "Call me crazy, but I'm gonna put money down that you're an eco-friendly gal. The condom in my pocket expires tomorrow. You wanna help me use it?"

I was seriously close to letting Fifi do her thing with my ex.

"No thanks," I said, keeping my voice at a higher register than normal. I didn't look like myself, but there was a chance my voice could give me away.

"Hey, Dave," Slash said. "Do I have ten minutes to play carpenter with Sunshine? First we'll get hammered, then I'll nail her."

The group laughed like they'd just heard a brilliant joke. The only joke was Slash the Rash.

"No can do, Boss Man," Dave told him. "Your ex is here somewhere and the dame who's paying for the gig is on her way back for a meet-and-greet."

"Fuck," Slash said, grabbing my hand and writing his number on my arm. "After the show. Me and you. I'm not a dentist, but believe you me, I'm gonna give you one hell of a filling, Sunshine."

Throat punching the pig was a bad move, but I was so close to violence I could taste it. As much as I knew I shouldn't engage, my mouth didn't sync up with my brain. "Don't bother," I said with a smile. "And just so you know, being a dick won't make yours any bigger."

Slash's eyes grew huge. His entourage laughed. "What did you say?"

"Whoops, my bad," I amended. "I meant to ask if your ass gets jealous of all the crap that comes out of your mouth?"

"Burn," Dave said with a bellow of laughter.

Slash Gordon didn't know what to make of what was happening. He wasn't smart enough. "Was that a joke?" he asked, wildly confused.

"For me to know and you to never find out," I replied as I tried to walk away.

The dumbass wasn't having it. He grabbed my hand and held it tight. "I like a gal who doesn't kiss my ass, Sunshine. Reminds me of my ex-wife. Oh, when she shows up, you're gonna have to skedaddle."

His grip was tight. I knew I could break it, but we'd drawn a crowd. I was a damned idiot. When would I learn to keep my mouth shut?

And then it went from mortifying to terrifying.

Every Demon in the backstage area dropped to their knees and pressed their foreheads to the black marble floor. The sudden movement created an ominous wind. The only people standing were human… and Fifi and me.

In a move so fast I almost missed it, Fifi elbowed Slash, causing him to lurch forward and release my hand. In a matter of a second, she and I were hidden behind an enormous ten-foot speaker. Dagon, Cher, Shiva and Ophelia were waiting for us. I was changing my mind about not wanting the Succubus around permanently. She was a badass of epic proportions.

"What's happening?" I whispered.

"Pandora," Ophelia mouthed and pointed to a slat in the speaker where we could watch and not be seen.

The sensual beat in the background was no longer in the background. It was front and center and I felt it with every part of my body—especially my reproductive parts. Quickly thinking about Candy Vargo's Angel-eating debacle, along with the fact that I'd had sex with Slash Gordon twenty years ago, I was able to repulse myself to a state that I could handle.

The Demons on the ground who were loyal to Pandora were not doing as well. They undulated and moaned. Many removed their clothing. It was disturbing and debasing. I noticed a few of Lilith's people playing along to fit in. At least I hoped they were playing along.

Holding my breath, I waited to see the woman who wanted my decapitated head.

She did not disappoint.

Ten flaming assholes proceeded her. Slash and his crew applauded wildly. They thought it was a trick. It was not.

Forming a circle around Slash and his group, all the flaming assholes took a knee.

"Now this is what I'm talking about," Slash shouted, high-fiving his buddies.

"Silence," one of the Demons roared. "You will speak when you are spoken to."

"No prob, dude," Slash replied with a huge grin. He made the international zip-the-lip sign and kept grinning. He had no clue of the danger he was in.

Pandora entered the area accompanied by Rhoda Spark and a bizarrely muted version of Abaddon. Seeing him made me feel breathless and agitated. Both women had a tight grip on one of his arms. Rhoda was almost naked and had her body pressed against his. The desire to rip her apart with my bare hands was strong.

Making sense of what was happening in my heart and head was impossible. All I knew was that I wanted to kill the two women who touched Abaddon against his will. I'd never been a bloodthirsty person in my forty years. I supposed there was a first time for everything. It was my lack of self-control that was most alarming.

The stupid and traitorous Rhoda gloated as she walked with her new Goddess and their hostage. She kicked at the writhing Demons who were in her way and rubbed herself like a cat in heat on Abaddon.

He was expressionless. His eyes were vacant and glazed over. The life seemed to have been sucked out of him. It made me feel panicky. The black suit he wore was expensive and he moved as if he was being compelled.

A low growl started deep in my throat. Dagon touched my shoulder and squeezed. "No. Not now."

I swallowed my fury and focused.

Pandora was so stunning it was almost difficult to look at her. However, there was an evil iciness to her that made me shudder. Her hair was raven black and hung in a shiny curtain to her waist. Her gown was a shimmering silver and her lips were a slash of blood red. The Demon moved as if she was floating on air.

"Fucking hell," Ophelia muttered. "She's cast a spell on Abaddon."

"Demons can cast spells?" I asked, feeling my chest tighten, making it difficult to breathe.

"Only Goddesses," she explained.

The wheels of my brain started spinning. "What kinds of spells?" I was a Goddess. Even though I didn't want to be, I was a freaking Goddess. The thoughts racing in my head were a chaotic hot mess, but I was a good story plotter. Rewriting crappy scenes had always been one of my superpowers as an actress. The show we were currently watching sucked. I was grabbing at straws, but if I didn't do something I was pretty sure I would go up in flames.

Ophelia shrugged. "I think any kind of spell they want."

That didn't help. I did a whole lot better with some direction. Could I turn Pandora into a bug and step on her? Could I blow up the building, grab Abaddon and get him out? Could I go invisible and trip the evil woman then escape with Abaddon?

I needed more clarification.

"Can a Goddess cast a spell on another Goddess?" I asked so quietly, I barely heard my question.

Dagon shook his head.

Okay, turning Pandora into a rodent and filling the place with hungry cats was a no-go.

"Abaddon's power is restored, but she's controlling it with black magic," Lilith ground out furiously.

I jumped and glanced around in surprise. Lilith wasn't with us.

"Did you hear that?" I asked Ophelia.

"Yes," she said, putting a finger to her lips to remind me to keep my voice low. "Our Goddess can speak to us."

"She's like a walkie-talkie?"

Dagon pressed his lips together and tried not to smile. "So to speak, yes."

"Can we talk back to her?" I asked.

Shiva shrugged. "Dagon can. Normally, Abaddon can. The rest of us cannot. You might be able to."

"I want ten of our people in the house. Ten backstage, and the

others will come to me," Lilith went on. *"On my command, you will burn this place to the ground along with everyone loyal to Pandora in it."*

Holy shit. My mother did not screw around.

"Ophelia, you will create a distraction shortly," Lilith commanded. *"I have to break the spell on Abaddon or he'll fight all of us to the death when we try to take him."*

"Not prudent," Dagon said without moving his lips. *"If you engage directly with Pandora, she will have cause to rule without you. Without the balance, all will be lost."*

Lilith's silence was loud. She didn't say a word, but I could feel her fury.

"I have to engage to break the spell," she said flatly. *"I refuse to leave him behind. Abaddon has been loyal to me since the beginning. He has not only saved my life, he also saved the life of my daughter."*

Dagon would not be silenced. *"Is one loyal subject worth risking the lives of all, my Goddess? Is that what Abaddon would want? I can assure you, I would not. I firmly believe he would not want that either."*

Again, she was silent. I didn't like the way the conversation was going. At all. They could leave. I wasn't going anywhere. There was no way I was leaving Abaddon in the clutches of the vicious whack job who was holding him hostage.

"I'm a Goddess," I stated, speaking the words intentionally inside my head. My lips didn't move.

No one said a word. However, it was clear that they heard me from the looks on Dagon's, Shiva's and Ophelia's faces. Fifi and Cher were clueless to the back and forth, but they weren't Demons.

I was.

"Lilith, you need to leave," I said.

Ophelia's eyes grew huge. Dagon stared at the floor. Only Shiva nodded with approval.

"I've got this."

My mother laughed. It pissed me off, but I didn't blame her. I'd been aware of my Demon status for a millisecond compared to the others here. My entire track record consisted of lopping off the heads of five flaming assholes. There were a lot more than five flaming assholes surrounding us, but I wasn't alone.

And I had a kinda-sorta plan. It was far better than leaving Abaddon here.

In an episode of *Camp Bite*, I'd saved my brother from the aliens from Planet 9. They'd probed his brain and had plans to dissect him for science. I wasn't having any of that crap. Nope. I'd rendered myself invisible, slashed my hand with my fangs, then snuck in when the aliens weren't looking. I fed three drops of my magical blood to Sean while the live studio audience cheered like crazy. The blood broke the extraterrestrials' control and we kicked some alien ass. Together. The way it was supposed to be.

I'd been a fictional vampire, but I was a very real Demon. The stakes were higher, but I was going to go with a version of what I knew.

I smiled as the words of Dagon and Lilith danced in my mind and made my chaotic thoughts linear. My mother had said to think of her blood as a boost… best when used for others. Her words were turning out to be prophetic. And Dagon had dropped the alarming truth bomb that the blood of a Goddess is more powerful than magic.

"Will my blood break the spell?" I asked.

Lilith's hissed intake of breath answered the question. Now

it was a matter of putting the scene together and adding costumes.

"I will not allow this," she snapped. *"It's a death wish."*

Pressing the bridge of my nose, I sighed. The woman didn't know me at all. *"I didn't ask permission,"* I shot back. *"From what I understand, if we try to save him without breaking the spell, he'll attack and end us. Correct?"*

"Yes," she replied in a clipped and pissed-off tone.

"Awesome," I said with an eye roll that she couldn't see but was pretty sure she knew about anyway. *"And if you get busted trying to break the spell, Pandora wins and Armageddon rolls on in?"*

"Something like that," she replied.

"Again, awesome," I said with sarcasm dripping off the words. *"As I would guess you already know, that shitbag Pandora put a bounty on my head. I'll be looking over my shoulder for the rest of my days. That's a given. What doesn't work for me is that my dad and brother are in grave danger because of that. Unacceptable. If I bite it saving the Demon who saved me, it's a win as far as I'm concerned. My dad and brother will fall off of her radar. If they don't, I ask that you protect them for the duration of their lives."*

Her sigh was loud. My eye roll was large.

"What is your plan?" she finally asked.

Dagon watched me with fascination. Ophelia watched me as if I was crazy. She wasn't wrong. Shiva was torn. She wanted to respect me, but it was killing her.

"My blood," I replied.

"Go on," Lilith pressed.

"We keep the Demons at the ready to blow this joint sky high. Dagon can make that call after I break the spell. I'll use Slash to get to Abaddon." I was pulling the plan out of my ass as I spoke and I wasn't quite sure where it was going. *"He thinks I'm a groupie."* I wanted to pace. It wasn't possible. Instead, I shoved my hands

into my pockets. A wide grin slowly spread across my lips as I felt the dagger Fifi had slipped in there. *"How much of my blood would Abaddon need to break the spell?"*

"Just a drop," Lilith replied.

"I can do this," I told her. I closed my eyes and pictured Man-mom and Sean. Leaving them would be devastating. But on the flip side, I knew I couldn't go on if something happened to them because of me. Strangely, I felt the same about Abaddon. It was absurd since we barely knew each other. *"I'm going to do this. There's a chance Pandora won't know who I am."*

"Doubtful," my mother said.

Needing another little plot bunny, I went for it. *"Is it possible for me to create a spell that makes me seem human?"*

"Do you hate me?" Lilith asked, clearly frustrated and at her wits end.

"I don't know you," I replied. *"You seem okay, but that's not on the table for discussion at the moment. I asked a question."*

"Yes. The answer is yes."

"How?" I asked.

Her voice was tight with tension. It matched the knots in my stomach.

"Wish it," she replied.

"That's it?" I asked, surprised. *"Just wish it and it will happen?"*

I glanced at Dagon. He had paled considerably. The Demon nodded his head.

"Yes" Lilith confirmed. *"Never use the gift unwisely, Cecily. Spells can destroy as much as aid. I will leave the building, but not the plane. Dagon's points were well made. I didn't expect Pandora to have obliterated so many of the age-old rules. Trapping one of my people to get to you is beyond the pale. She's gone too far this time, but it's not under my jurisdiction to punish her."*

"Who can punish her?"

"*Candy Vargo,*" she replied.

Dagon, Ophelia and Shiva shuddered. I didn't. Candy Vargo was A-freaking-okay in my book—toothpicks and shitty pole dancing included.

"*Works for me,*" I said, pulling a toothpick out of my pocket and kissing it.

Forty was young to end it all, but forty-one would suck hard if I didn't try to save Abaddon.

"*You're not willing to back down?*" Lilith tried one more time.

"*I'm not.*"

"*Cecily, this is wrong,*" she insisted. "*You don't know what you're doing or who you're dealing with.*"

"*Do you want to leave Abaddon here?*" I demanded.

"*I do not.*"

"*Neither do I,*" I said in a flat tone. "*I'll do what needs to be done.*"

"*Promise me this,*" she said. "*Once the spell has been broken, you will leave the building. You must give me your word.*"

It was a reasonable request. I'd never been in a real battle with a shitload of Demons. The reality of that was chilling. Once Abaddon was back to himself, I knew he could handle it. Plus, there were at least thirty others here who would have his back.

"*You have my word, Lilith,*" I told her.

"*Then you have my blessing, child. I understand your compulsion even if you do not.*"

I liked the blessing part. The compulsion part—not as much. I wasn't being forced to do anything. It was my choice. Whatever. Hopefully, the blessing meant that her posse of Demon protectors would back me up.

"*You're a Goddess, Cecily,*" she said softly. "*From this moment *forward, there is no denying it or going back. Follow your heart and your gut. I'll be waiting for you."*

Dagon, Ophelia, Shiva, Fifi and Cher were all staring at me. Fifi and Cher were calm. The other three were not. Strangely, I was more at peace than I'd ever been in my life.

"Cher, can you make me up to look like a groupie and magic me up a slutty outfit?"

"Darn tootin'," she replied, pulling out her makeup bag.

"Ophelia, are you cool with showing some boob?" I asked.

"Sure thing, bitch," she replied with a thumbs up. "One or both?"

"Both," I confirmed.

"My liege." Fifi lifted her shirt and exposed her girls. "I too can flash mammary. I have an outstanding rack."

"Ohhhh," Ophelia said with admiration. "Are those real?"

"No," Fifi replied. "Do you want the name of the surgeon?"

"Hell to the yes," she said, fist bumping the Succubus.

I peeked out of the slat and almost snarled. Rhoda was literally humping Abaddon's leg. Quickly looking away, I pointed at Cher.

I used her words that were fast becoming our motto. "Let's get this party started."

CHAPTER TWELVE

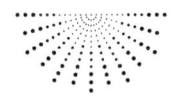

"You look like a hooker," Ophelia said with approval.

I grimaced. "Thank you."

Cher worked fast as I caught her and Fifi up on the conversation I'd had with Lilith. I was overly made up and wearing a mini skirt and halter top that showed not only side boob but bottom butt as well. I'd opted to keep my black combat boots on. They were totally trendy and I could run better in them than heels.

"Plan?" Shiva whispered.

I pulled them in close. "I'm going to beeline for Slash pretending to be wasted. I'm terrific at pratfalls."

"Damn straight," Cher said. "Better than a stunt woman. Cecily always does her own stunts unless insurance prohibits it. My gal jumped off two five-story buildings in a Lifetime movie. She was being chased by Quakers. Great stuff. Brought a tear to my eye."

"Impressive, my liege Cecily," Fifi said.

I blushed. Cher was like a proud mom on crack. I adored her and her belief in me. The movie had been awful, but my stunts and the paycheck had been killer. "Thanks. As I pass Abaddon, I'll wipe out. Bingo, bango, bongo. I've played wasted plenty of times. I've got that crap down."

"That's it?" Dagon asked, alarmed.

"What do you mean?" I asked.

Dagon winced. "I hope you left a lot of that plan out."

"Whoops. That I did," I said, cupping the dagger in my hand and holding it to my side so it was hidden. "I'm going to pierce my hand and make it bleed before we go out there. When I fall, I'll stab Abaddon in the leg or foot then slap my hand over the wound. Lilith said it only takes a drop. The plan is to be such a wasted bimbo that no one will notice what I've done."

"How are my boobs playing into this?" Ophelia asked.

"And mine?" Fifi added, pointing at her perky pair.

"You're my drunk buddies," I explained. Cher quickly waved her hand and dressed the gals similarly to me. We looked like working girls. "Stick close. When we get near them, start fighting. Get Rhoda out of the way."

"Still not getting how my tits figure in," Ophelia said, sounding disappointed.

I paused and mulled it over. "I guess they don't."

"Actually," Fifi interjected, "stupendous knockers like Ophelia's and mine would enhance the chaos. My melons have caused traffic accidents and started wars. Try this plan on for size… We stagger out in front of you, screaming for the loser rock star. When we get near Abaddon, Ophelia punches me in the face so she can reach the spandex-wearing shitass first. It will be fine if you break my nose. I'm getting it done in two weeks."

Ophelia nodded. "That works for me. Stay away from my teeth. I just got veneers. What about our knockers?"

"Getting to that," Fifi assured her. "I get so furious that you broke my nose, I tear your shirt off in a rage. You scream and get pissed while tearing my shirt off in retribution. Then, I'll lose my mind and head butt your prodigious and exposed bosom. The move will give you the velocity needed to fly into Rhoda and knock her away. I'll then tackle you and we can go to town. Cecily does her thing while we create the distraction."

"Love it," Ophelia announced. "I say we beat the living daylights out of Rhoda too. Nothing would give me more pleasure than dismembering her. If the backstabbing bitch has no appendages, it will be easier to deliver her to the Goddess Lilith."

My mouth was open. That was a lot. However, in a batshit crazy way it made sense. Fifi had taken a pass at rewriting the scene and made it better. Ophelia had added the final touches. Granted it definitely jumped the shark, but if we were going to die, we might as well go out in style.

Dagon seemed somewhat shocked by the scheme, but found his voice quicker than I did. "While I must admit I'm a bit flabbergasted, I actually think that might work."

"You do?" I asked.

Cher chimed in. "It's so fucking insane, I believe it will. Can you spell the three of you to seem human without actually becoming human?"

It was the million-dollar question. I peeked out again. Pandora was holding court with Slash. He was kissing her ass and hitting on her. I overheard the vile Goddess asking Slash about his ex-wife… who would be me. It was a blessing that he could honestly say that he hadn't seen me here. She was not pleased. She was about to be less pleased.

Abaddon was still in a daze and Rhoda was still all over him.

Not for much longer.

All I had to do was wish. Being specific was important.

"Umm... do I say the spell out loud or just to myself?" I asked.

Everyone looked like deer caught in headlights. I was horrified that I hadn't asked Lilith for the spell particulars.

"It's fifty-fifty," Cher said, putting lipstick on her eyelids. "I'm going with out loud."

I nodded then groaned. "Should it rhyme?"

Again, no one knew.

Shit.

"Couldn't hurt," Shiva said, looking wildly unsure.

"Rhyming and out loud," I muttered.

Here went nothing...

Closing my eyes tight, I sent the wish into the Universe. Improv wasn't my thing. I liked to write and revise. There was no time for that. I crossed my fingers and let it rip.

"To whom it may concern, this wish is for the Demon Ophelia, the Succubus Fifi and myself—the Demon Goddess Cecily," I began, feeling all kinds of insecure and ridiculous. However, I figured a polite intro was a respectful way to start. It was also important to clarify who the hell I was wishing for. First part done. Second, on its way.

"Death is loomin' and we need to appear human. But we must keep our power or the plan will go sour." My rhyming was shitty, but it didn't stop me. "There's a bad Demon schemein' who wants my dead head. Pandora's a whore-a, her evil mustn't spread." I winced at the whore reference, but once I'd said her name, I had to come up with something. "It's unacceptable that we're wrecked, the spell must protect. With my friends, we will defend and the wickedness shall end." The last part had to put some kind of time stamp on it. "So much is at stake. The spell must last until the evil enchantment I break. Thank you and have a good day."

Everyone was silent for an entire minute. It felt like an eternity. I wasn't sure how to take the reaction. My face heated up and I started to feel defensive. How much better could they have done under pressure?

"Oscar worthy," Cher said, kissing my cheek.

I heaved out a relieved sigh. Granted, Cher thought everything I did was Oscar worthy, but right now, I would take it.

"You really can fly," Ophelia whispered reverently.

"Not sure it worked," I said, still feeling kind of itchy for creating a string of shitastic rhymes. I inhaled deeply and did what I had to do. I squinted my eyes at Ophelia and Fifi. Neither glowed. I almost cried with relief. Turning to Dagon, I waited for his judgement.

The Demon squinted his eyes at me then broke into a smile. "It worked." He then turned serious. "Fifi, you must remove Cecily from the building when the spell on Abaddon has been broken. Ophelia, you will get all of the humans out. Am I clear?"

"Crystal," Ophelia said.

The Succubus saluted Dagon. "Perfectly clear. I will ferry my liege to safety with great haste when she has completed her mission."

Dagon saluted Fifi back.

"Are we ready?" I asked, feeling my heart pound like a jackhammer in my chest.

The sensation was far more intense than the butterflies I usually felt before a performance. Not surprising. Showbusiness was fake. This was not.

"I say we get this party started!" Fifi announced, tucking a few knives into her boots.

"You know, we should really get some t-shirts made with that saying on them," Ophelia mused aloud. "We seem to use it a lot."

"Done deal," I promised as I purposely cut my palm with the knife. "We just have to live through the party first."

~

Our entrance was loud and obnoxious. We gelled like we'd worked together on multiple TV projects. Fifi as a drunk was so freaking realistic, I wondered if she'd secretly downed a bottle of vodka when I wasn't looking. Ophelia staggered like she was about to go down. I was right behind her.

"Slash Gordon! I love you!" Fifi squealed at a pitch so high I almost slapped my hands over my ears.

That would have been tragic considering I was carrying a dagger. Stabbing myself in the head before I'd finished the scene was not in the script.

"He's mine," Ophelia shouted, shoving Fifi aside as she clumsily ran towards our goal.

All eyes were on us. Even the Demons on the floor peeked up at the commotion. Thankfully, no one seemed concerned since we were *human*. However, they were annoyed. Pandora's expression screwed up with displeasure, but not one Demon made a move to stop or harm us.

Dagon had promised that Demons were not allowed to kill humans under any circumstances. I crossed my fingers and hoped that would hold true.

"He's mine, whore," Fifi bellowed at Ophelia. "I get to bang him first and if you're lucky I'll give you sloppy seconds. But trust me, he won't be able to walk for a week when I get done riding him."

The Demons were amused. Even Pandora began to enjoy the show.

"She's got the crabs," Ophelia screamed, slapping haphazardly at Fifi to throw her off course. "Slash, don't bang her. BANG ME! I have great tits and a disease-free vagina."

The Demons were now laughing at the silly *humans*. My gals had them in the palms of their hands.

"LIAR," Fifi snarled. "But to be on the safe side, I'll just blow you."

"She's like a Hoover vacuum," Ophelia yelled. "She'll rip your love-stick right off your body with the suction. Don't do it, Slash! Your salami is perfection!"

Fifi's shriek of horror sent the laughing audience of deadly Demons into hysterics. It was all I could do not to join them. I couldn't have written more appalling or perfect dialogue.

"Wrong," I slurred as I pushed my way forward. "I'm his Sunshine. He wants me."

"Is that you, Sunshine?" Slash asked, confused. "Holy shit! You're rock-hard boner material, babe. How about I bang all of you? You first, of course."

"Just me," I insisted, over-enunciating my words like a good drunk would.

As I stumbled forward, I caught Abaddon's unfocused gaze. His eyes widened in recognition then began to blaze a furious red.

Shit. He was spelled by Pandora. How was he able to recognize me? I didn't look anything like my normal self. His hands formed fists at his side, and he looked like he wanted to kill. Not me. He wanted to kill Slash. That was not good. Demons weren't permitted to kill humans. I had no clue what the punishment for that might be, but I didn't want to find out.

The pace of the scene needed to pick up or we were all going down in flames.

"Oh my GOD! Slash!" I squealed as I sprinted like my ass was on fire.

Ophelia and Fifi were not stupid. They followed my lead and began beating the daylights out of each other. The Demons were thrilled. Money was being thrown down on the floor and bets were being taken.

Fifi and Ophelia took their roles seriously and in a matter of seconds, they'd knocked Rhoda out of the way and went to town on each other and her.

Rhoda's rage was like nothing I'd ever seen. She lit up like a Christmas tree on steroids and went at the *humans* with a vengeance that made me worry for the safety of my friends.

"You will die," she screeched as she dove at Ophelia and Fifi. "No one fucks with RHODA SPARK!"

The plot twist wasn't good. I was about to do a quick rewrite in my head, but didn't have to. Pandora ended up having my back. I couldn't have predicted the next thirty seconds if I'd tried.

"Stupid wench. You've ground my last nerve," Pandora snarled, raising her perfectly manicured hands high. "They're human. OFF LIMITS. And you, Rhoda Spark... are dead."

The evil Goddess slashed her arms down and Rhoda literally blew up. Her guts went flying and her detached head rolled a few feet before it went up in flames and exploded. The Demons cheered. Slash and his entourage turned and ran like the devil was on their heels out of the building. I vomited in my mouth. Thankfully, the humans were now safe. One less thing for Ophelia to do.

The chaos gave me an opening and I needed to take it quick. Spelled or not, Abaddon moved to go after Slash and his idiots. His murderous glare was stomach churning. Pandora was preening and taking rabid delight in the assassination she'd just committed and had momentarily forgotten about her hostage. Perfect. Dagon had been correct. Her arrogance would be her undoing.

Taking a page out of the most embarrassing audition of my career, which had resulted in stitches and new teeth, I dove at Abaddon like I could fly. Thinking on my feet, I made it look like I'd slipped on Rhoda's guts and lost my footing. Truthfully, I did slip on her guts but used the repulsive mishap like a seasoned actress would.

Aiming for his leg, I stabbed it. It felt every kind of wrong to maim him and the sound was gross. Real life was much more disturbing than showbiz—especially when one happened to be a Demon. Never in my wildest dreams would I have considered stabbing someone who I wanted to date… until today. Under more normal circumstances, planting a knife in a potential lover would end in a restraining order, some jail time, community service and shitty press that would require a full-time publicist to spin it into something palatable for the viewing public. Not today.

The knife sliced through his pants and embedded in his calf. Blood spurted everywhere. I was so happy, I almost cried. I'd have to save the tears for later. The cameras were still rolling and the scene wasn't over. There was no time for a second take. We had to nail the first one. Abaddon's expression was one of utter shock as he stopped his forward motion and glared down at me.

"What the fuck?" he hissed, trying to kick me away.

I wasn't having it. His eyes were still glazed over and he wasn't himself. The Demon struggled to recognize me and seemed confused as to why he was chasing Slash.

"Hang tight, Dick," I whispered as I slapped my bleeding hand over the wound and held fast.

Abaddon's body convulsed violently as the spell broke. His eyes rolled back in his head and his huge body dropped to the ground next to me with a thud. I was shocked and beyond relieved that all the attention was on Pandora and no one seemed to notice what had just happened. His breathing was labored. If he was human, I'd think he was having a heart attack or a stroke. Abaddon was not human. Although, right now, he seemed like a wild animal about to snap.

I crawled away a few feet just in case this turned into a kill-the-messenger kind of scenario. It would be some messed-up karma if he offed me after practically dying for me.

Thankfully, his bewilderment only lasted a few more seconds. Then the situation flipped and went from scary to sexual. The scene had taken on a life of its own and was writing itself.

Abaddon's eyes hooded with intense desire. The Demon had gone from wanting to kill me to wanting to do me. He pulled me against his hard body and kissed me as if both our lives depended on it. The kiss was urgent and bizarrely necessary. His lips moved seductively against mine and I melted into him willingly. Our tongues tangled and a tingle shot all the way to my toes. The taste of him on my lips was addictive. Everything around me ceased to exist for a brief moment. Now, I struggled to catch my breath.

The kiss was life-altering. The aftermath, not so much.

Abaddon got mad. Really mad. Furiously mad. He pulled the dagger out of his leg and stared at it.

"What the hell did you do, Cecily?" he snapped.

I was jerked back into the ugly reality—and it was some serious ugly. "Saved your ass, Dick," I informed him, using the name I'd given him when we'd met due to his shitty demeanor and attitude. "A thank you would be lovely."

"You should not be here," he growled. His eyes were wild as he scanned the area.

"Well, I'm here. Deal with it, jackass," I shot right back.

Maybe my blood hadn't removed all of the spell.

"If I hadn't sworn to protect you, I would kill you," he ground out. "You have no business being here. It's too dangerous. You could die. That's unacceptable."

I was tempted to point out that he'd just threatened to kill me himself, but held back.

He glanced warily over his shoulder again. Pandora was still accepting accolades for her murderous behavior. She was surrounded by her people. His gaze returned to me and he growled.

I couldn't hold back anymore. My mouth was way ahead of my common sense. "Go ahead," I dared him. "Kill me. It would solve a whole lot of problems for you and your people."

His eyes narrowed to slits. "You are one of my *people* and I want you out of here. Now," Abaddon commanded.

I punched him in the stomach. It didn't even faze him. I had the worst taste in men. Abaddon had saved me. I'd paid him back. I was done with him. "On my way, asshole."

As if on cue, Fifi showed up and pulled me to my feet. Abaddon snarled and moved to end her. I sent a small electrocution his way with a wiggle of my fingers. "She's on our team. Do *not* harm her or I'll whip up my purple fire sword and make you a soprano."

"A Succubus is on our team?" he asked, ignoring my threat and the fact that I'd just sent electricity through him.

"Yes," I hissed. "Lilith knows. Your Goddess wants this building and everyone loyal to Pandora destroyed. She wants me gone for that part. My goal was to break the spell. I did that."

Dagon, Ophelia and Shiva appeared in a puff of red mist at our side.

"We must make our move now," Dagon insisted, extending his hand to Abaddon. "The others are ready."

Abaddon nodded curtly to Fifi. "Get her out of here. NOW."

Fifi grabbed me and tossed me over her shoulder. She sprinted like she was an Olympic runner going for a world record. My stomach plummeted as Pandora's screams of fury bounced and echoed ominously when she realized that the spell on Abaddon had been broken.

"The Demon Abaddon does not leave this building alive," she bellowed then waved her hands in a circular motion.

I watched in horror as she disappeared in a flash of glittering red and black that killed many of the people surrounding her. She was a shitty leader. Where Lilith refused to leave one of her people behind, Pandora killed her own to save her ass. However, it didn't seem to bother them. Her remaining army of about a hundred Demons narrowed in on Abaddon and his crew.

Abaddon's roar of savagery beat Pandora's hands down. Fifi swore as Pandora's henchmen blocked our exit. It wasn't clear if they knew who I was, but asking was out of the question. The Succubus turned on a dime and ran for another door leading outside. Each one was blocked by flaming assholes. I was beginning to think we might be screwed.

"Son of a bitch," Fifi choked out. "I don't know how to get us out of this shithole. I'm failing you, my liege."

"Put me down," I insisted, beating on her back. "We have to fight."

The Succubus did as I asked. We backed ourselves up against a wall so no one could come at us from behind. The entire concert hall was chaotic mayhem—screams and shouts permeated the air. Shockingly, no one seemed to be after us. They were going for Abaddon as per the instructions of their hideous Goddess. However, some stayed back and all the exits were blocked.

I was breaking my promise to Lilith. Getting out of here didn't look like an option. I never broke promises, but this one had become impossible to fulfill.

The sheer amount of magic flying all over the place made it difficult to breathe. I watched as those loyal to Lilith transported to Abaddon in the center of the bedlam. The movies got Demons all wrong. Nothing I'd ever seen on the silver screen came close to the bloodcurdling scene being played out. The Demon who I'd thought I was falling for looked like the Angel of Death—his eyes blazed a sparkling bloody red and power vibrated from his body. There was nothing even remotely human about him. It was flat out the most terrifying thing I'd ever witnessed. The batshit crazy part of me found it disturbingly beautiful. I was going to need so much therapy if I lived until tomorrow.

The Demons joined hands and black fire exploded out of them with a pop that I was certain had busted my eardrums. Wind ripped through the cavernous hall. I grabbed onto a pole so I didn't get blown into the fray. A crack of thunder boomed as the crystal chandeliers fell from the rafters and shattered into millions of tiny shimmering pieces.

"We need to boogie," Cher huffed out as she poofed in next to us. "Lots of people about to die."

"No clear exit," Fifi said frantically.

Without conscious thought, I cast a spell. "To whom it may

concern," I whispered in a panic, pulling Cher and Fifi close. "This spell is for Cher the Angel, Fifi the Succubus and myself, Cecily the Demon Goddess. Protect us from the trouble. Put us in an impenetrable bubble. NOW. Bubble, please stay until the evil goes away. Thank you and have a good day."

In the time it took to blink, an iridescent bubble surrounded us.

"Hot damn, girlfriend," Cher said, patting me on the back. "You're a badass!"

I didn't feel like a badass. Badasses didn't get scared. I was terrified. It was glaringly obvious why Lilith hadn't wanted me here for this part. If this was my new life, I didn't want it. I wasn't cut out for this kind of shit.

What happened next, I wouldn't wish on my worst enemy. The raging black fire coming from Lilith's Demons morphed into crackling, elongated tendrils of flame—almost rope-like. Abaddon controlled the flames and directed them like he was conducting a lethal orchestra. They zipped through the air and chased those loyal to Pandora. The flaming assholes did their best to fight back, but they were no match for the sheer deadly power coming from Abaddon and his people.

In a language I didn't understand, Abaddon chanted and raised his strong arms high. As he slashed them to his sides, the ropes found their prey and lassoed themselves around the necks of those who had been party to the heinous crimes of Pandora. The screams of fury and terror made my stomach roil. Demons were a violent species. Another boom of thunder followed by a crack of lightning blasted as every single one of Pandora's flaming assholes were decapitated and burned to ash.

It was over for now. I wasn't naïve enough to believe this was a one and done.

The bubble protecting us disintegrated and fell in a glittering powder at our feet.

"Holy fuck," Fifi muttered. "Impressive."

"And then some," Cher agreed.

My agent's entire face was covered in orange lipstick. She was gorgeous.

It was good there was nothing left in my stomach. If there had been, I would have lost it.

Scanning the area quickly, I spotted Abaddon, Dagon, Ophelia, Shiva and the others. They were fine—bloody but fine. I was not. My body shook violently. "I want to get out of here," I whispered.

Fifi bowed to me. "As you wish, my liege."

Without any fanfare or notice, we slipped out of the building. Fifi guided us to the sedan, got behind the wheel and hauled ass out of the parking lot. The explosion behind us wasn't unexpected. Turning to look out of the back windshield, I stared at the inferno that used to be the Golden Showers Bet and Bed. Soon there would be nothing left of the casino. If there was no proof, there was no crime. It depressed me that I felt a visceral affinity to the blaze. It angered me that I was losing myself in the crazy. I didn't want to find the Darkness appealing or sexy.

But I did.

That was going to be a problem.

CHAPTER THIRTEEN

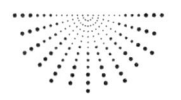

Fifi drove expertly but at a speed that made me grip the dashboard in fear. It would suck to die in a car accident after what we'd just survived. Cher sat calmly in back and wiped the lipstick off of her face. It was all I could do not to beg the Succubus to slow down.

"Where are we going?" I did my best to keep my voice steady.

"Back to Sushi's club. It's safe there," Fifi said. "There are others waiting for us."

"Who?" I asked, looking down at my blood-and-guts-covered hooker outfit and wincing. "And how do you know that?"

Fifi kept her eyes on the road. "Sushi texted me. I don't know who is there. However, there is good news."

"I would love some good news," I told her with a weak laugh.

The Succubus smiled. "I've been given permission by Sushi to become your permanent bodyguard. I have not fornicated with anyone in four centuries and can be trusted not to kill randomly for sexual pleasure. It will be my life's work to keep my liege from harm."

My definition of good news was a little different than hers but I didn't say a word. Honestly, she was growing on me. I trusted her and I liked her even though she was nuts. I had to admit, four hundred years without sex for pleasure was monumental. However, 24/7 with Fifi might become an issue. If she kept offering to bang my enemies to death, we were going to have to have a serious discussion. I was also kind of iffy about keeping grenades in my home.

"Is Sushi some kind of Succubus president?" I inquired. The hierarchy of the Immortals was a big mystery. I was curious why Fifi had to get Sushi's permission.

"She's our queen," Fifi said with great reverence.

And the world kept getting crazier. I'd known Sushi half my life as one of the top costume designers in Hollywood. I was pretty sure she'd won a few Emmys and had even been nominated for an Oscar. Her specialty was historical costumes… which now made perfect sense since she'd lived through all those eras.

"You're gonna love LA," Cher told Fifi. "Tell you what, I'll rep you. You could have a killer career playing an assassin in action flicks. You're beautiful, badass and have a wonderful bosom."

"As long as it doesn't interfere with eliminating Cecily's foes, then yes. I would find it quite satisfying to be an action star. However, I do not do sex scenes for obvious reasons. I would feel terrible about sucking the life force out of The Rock or Keanu Reeves. I understand Keanu is a very kind man. In fact, for that reason alone, I refuse to work with him. Accidently offing a soul as beautiful as his would depress me. I tend to get plastic surgery when I'm depressed. Not good."

"I'll make a note of that," Cher promised, pulling out her laptop and typing away. "Are you attracted to Arnold Schwarzenegger or Sylvester Stallone?"

"Absolutely not," she replied.

Cher kept typing. "Got it."

Was everyone nuts? I was going with a yes on that. My curiosity as to who was waiting for us made me feel wonky. Sushi had mentioned something about royalty earlier as her reason for staying back. Was I about to meet a bunch of Succubus princes and princesses? Or dukes and duchesses? My life had jumped the shark.

"Cher, can you magic me up a more respectable outfit, please?" I asked.

"Sure can," she said, snapping her laptop shut. "Do you want me to remove the guts from your hair?"

I gagged. I wanted no reminder of Rhoda Spark and I certainly didn't want to be wearing the guts of the awful Demon. "Yes," I choked out. "Can you also make me look like me again?"

She grinned and handed me a mirror from her bottomless bag. "You already do," she said. "The disguises wore off once we left the building."

She was correct. I was so busy silently freaking out about Fifi's driving, I hadn't noticed. Working on being more aware was top on my to-do list. If I was going to be running for my life on the regular, I couldn't be ignorant of my surroundings. If I died, I'd be pissed if it was because I'd been careless.

"So," Fifi said with a naughty grin. "You and Abaddon?"

I gave her the side eye. "I'm not sure. It's new. And my track record with men sucks."

"Tell me about it," she said with a groan.

I laughed. It was so absurd I couldn't help myself. "Anyhoo, I'm sure I'll screw it up. It's one of my superpowers."

"Doubtful," Cher said. "Probably impossible."

I glanced back at her. She smiled and winked. It was as if she knew something I didn't. Just as I was about to ask, Ophelia poofed into the backseat of the car.

I screamed. Fifi pulled out a grenade then put it back when she saw it was her busty drinking buddy. Cher just chuckled.

"I was AMAZING," Ophelia shouted. "Did you see me?"

"You did a good job," Cher told her, patting her on the head.

"Of course, I did," Ophelia said with her usual lack of humility. "I'm a badass. So, where are we headed? Back to LA?"

My heart was pounding like a jackhammer in my chest from my idiot buddy's unexpected arrival. The poofing thing was startling. I wasn't sure I'd ever get used to it. "Back to Sushi's club," I told her. "There are others waiting for us."

"Who?" she asked as she texted the information to Dagon.

"Not a clue."

Cher looked Ophelia over and shook her head. "Can't have my clients looking like streetwalkers." With a wave of her hand, Fifi, Ophelia and I were now sporting black Prada from head to toe.

My ensemble consisted of a gorgeous fitted knee-length dress, a decadently soft cashmere sweater and sky-high heels. I loved it. It was comfortable and chic. It screamed of cool confidence. If I couldn't be it, I could wear it. I was an excellent pretender.

"Is anyone else exhausted?" I asked, yawning.

"Pooped," Cher agreed. "I'll bet Sushi will put us up for the night again. That suite was over-the-top fan-freaking-tastic."

I leaned back in the seat and closed my eyes. Hopefully, the meet-and-greet would go fast. I didn't want to be rude, but I could fall asleep standing up.

"Sushi will most certainly welcome you," Fifi assured us. "She will insist. It's too late to go back to LA this evening."

"We could poof," Ophelia reminded us.

"How do you poof?" I asked, curious about the weird mode of Immortal transportation.

"Just visualize where you want to go," Ophelia explained. "Shall we?"

"Nope," I said. "I poofed with Abaddon once. It wasn't fun. I vote for driving back in the morning."

Fifi glanced over and smiled. "As you wish, my liege."

I smiled back. It would probably take some work, but she was going to have to drop the *my liege* thing. My name was Cecily. It was a perfectly good and normal name. Granted, in the last week or so I'd gone from normal to abnormal at warp speed, but I needed to hang on to some of the things that made me feel like me. My name was one of them.

I was too tired to get into it now. Reserving my energy for the *royalty* was all I could muster up. We'd deal with the name game tomorrow.

∽

I'D EXPECTED SOME KIND OF POMP.

I'd expected some kind of circumstance.

I'd expected crowns and possibly footmen.

What I got was nothing like I'd expected.

We were ushered to the private room at the back of the casino upon our arrival by some official-looking, armed-to-the-teeth Succubi. I knew their species by the white tuxes and shiny red patent leather shoes. They were all business. It made my nervousness ramp up substantially.

"Welcome," Sushi said warmly as we entered the room.

I paused at the door and examined the occupants. Some I knew. Some I didn't. It was abundantly clear they were all insanely powerful. The room literally vibrated with magic. They seemed to have divided themselves into camps and were cautiously tolerating each other.

I had no clue what game was being played, but I could tell the stakes were high.

My gaze landed on Abaddon's. He stared back at me with an intensity that made me uncomfortable. It wasn't clear if it was fury or lust. My gut instinct was to run to him for comfort and protection. I shoved my instinct away. His expression then closed off for the most part. For a moment, I saw the man I'd been falling for, but it was so brief, I convinced myself I'd imagined it.

My love life—or lack of one—was immaterial right now. Although, when I pulled my gaze from his, the Demon strode across the room and stood by my side. It felt right and wrong. This entire meeting seemed like some kind of pissing match where I was the prize.

Gideon, aka Uncle Grim Reaper, stood on the far left of the room. He was an imposing figure. However, he smiled at me. His beauty was obnoxious, but the woman next to him made him seem a little pale in comparison. Beside him stood his partner, Daisy, the Angel of Mercy and the one who aided the dead. She was stunning and nodded to me politely. Next to her stood a pretty woman with a pixie haircut. She had moving tattoos on her arms that seemed to be alive. It was wild.

There was a gentleman accompanying them with icy blue eyes. He terrified me even though his smile was kind. A different man wearing a mail-carrier's uniform was with them as well. And rounding out the group was Candy Vargo. She'd dressed up for the occasion. The toothpick-loving nutjob wore a dress. She was also sporting ratty tennis shoes, but it was the effort that counted.

The Grim Reaper's crew was intimidating. They were a mixed bag of different species. My guess was that most of them were regular Immortals—the kind that Cher said to steer clear of. I would keep the warning in mind.

Sushi stood with a group of Succubi in the center of the room. Aside from Sushi, they were all expressionless and had their hands on their weapons.

That didn't bode well. Had I walked into my execution? I sure as hell hoped not. I had to be at work on Monday.

On the far right were the Demons. Lilith stood front and center. She wore a sparkling red diaphanous gown that made her look like a Goddess personified. Her beauty was not of this world. Her expression was neutral. If she was pissed that I hadn't kept my promise, she could shove it. In the end, I was glad I'd seen what had gone down. I knew for sure I wanted no part of their violent existence.

With her stood Dagon and Shiva. Their expressions were as shuttered as their Goddess's. It made me feel small and stupid. I'd thought we were friends. Well, at least Dagon.

I looked to my right at Abaddon. He stared straight ahead. When would I stop being attracted to bad boys? We shared a physical attraction, but that was it. This time I was getting out before I got burned. The thought made my heart ache, but I was leading with my brain from now on.

Ophelia moved to stand with her Goddess.

Fifi and Cher stayed with Abaddon and me.

"Where do you stand, Cecily?" Sushi asked.

I squinted at her. What the hell was she talking about?

"Umm... right here," I replied. Was this some kind of test?

Sushi chuckled and shook her head. "Which group in the room do you prefer to stand with?"

I glanced around. My mother's eyes implored me to join her. It annoyed me. I didn't know her. Most of me trusted her, but a part of me didn't. Gideon raised a brow in question when I met his level gaze. I didn't know him either. We'd met once. Granted, he'd given me the gift to control my magic, but he was still basically a stranger to me. Plus, he had people in his group who I'd never seen before.

It was a given I wouldn't go with the Succubi. While I had traits in common with both Lilith's and Gideon's groups, I shared nothing familiar with the Succubi. Sucking the life force out of sexual partners or celibacy wasn't my thing.

Follow my gut. I'd been given the advice repeatedly. "I stand right here. On my own," I replied.

Lilith looked down at the floor. Abaddon tensed beside me. Gideon watched me as if I was a science experiment that was about to go seriously wrong. Only Candy Vargo seemed to be cool with my answer.

"Biggest fuckin' balls I've ever seen," she said, tossing me a box of toothpicks. "Cecily Bloom is a badass motherfucker."

While I didn't necessarily agree, I accepted the profane compliment with a smile and a nod her way. Catching the box easily in my hand, I took one out and put it into my mouth.

Both Gideon's and Lilith's brows shot up high. I thought I noticed Abaddon's lips quirk, but it was quick and I couldn't be sure. The jackass was still pissed at me. Whatever. I didn't like him all that much at the moment either. I still wanted the horrible man with every fiber of my being, but I definitely didn't like him right now.

I was tired. This was unsettling. It was time to get to the reason why they'd all gathered and then go to bed. It had been a long and grossly eventful day. "So, what's the occasion?"

Candy Vargo chuckled. "Badass motherfucker."

Sushi shot Candy a look. The Keeper of Fate zipped it quick.

The man in the mail uniform stepped forward and smiled. He seemed very socially awkward, but sweet. Immediately, he made me more comfortable.

"My name is Tim," he said. "I'm the Immortal Courier between the Darkness and the Light."

I was sure it had been a guy named Tim who got his legs amputated by Candy Vargo in a chariot race. I didn't dare ask. Candy and he were obviously friends now. If they were fine with it, who was I to judge? "Nice to meet you, Tim," I said politely, still not sure what was going down. "And you're here because?"

"We wanted to meet you because you're the newly emerged Goddess of the Darkness," he replied.

I squinted at him and tried to figure out what he was getting at. "So, umm… you deliver my mail?"

I regretted the question the moment it left my lips.

Gideon threw his head back and laughed. Candy Vargo literally fell to the floor, she was cackling so hard. Lilith and crew tried to hide their mirth. All of them failed miserably. Even Sushi and her band of armed Succubi were chuckling.

I was not. Embarrassment made me defensive. Only Abaddon seemed pissed on my behalf. Considering he was on my shitlist right now, it didn't matter.

"Oh, and about that Goddess thing," I said in my outdoor voice over the laughter. Everyone quieted immediately. I took the toothpick out of my mouth and tossed it aside. "I don't want the job. I'm an actress. No more, no less. I'm not cut out to be a Goddess. So thanks, but nope. Nice meeting everyone, kind of. I'm tired and want to go to sleep."

Lilith shook her head. Her eyes burned a bright and displeased red. I seriously hoped she wasn't about to have a go at me. "It's not that simple, child."

"I have a name," I told her emotionlessly. "Please use it. While you might have given birth to me, I'm not your child. I'm my father's daughter."

Daisy quickly stepped forward and took my hands in hers. "No one wants to harm you, Cecily," she promised.

"Can you relay that to Pandora?" I asked.

She looked back over her shoulder at Candy Vargo. "Candy, can you field the question, please?"

"Sure as fuck can," she said, crossing the room and standing nose to nose with me. "You make me proud, motherfucker."

"Thanks," I said. For being such a hot scary mess, she was nice.

"Pandora is in a time-out, so to speak," she said with a dastardly grin.

"Wanna be more specific?" I asked.

Candy put six toothpicks into her mouth. "Not sure you can handle the truth."

"Oh my God," I shouted. "Did you eat her?"

Everyone in the room gasped and backed away. The Succubi were positively green. For a bunch of Immortal badasses, they were weenies where Candy Vargo was concerned. I was halfway in and halfway out of the weenie camp. It did occur to me that I should be more afraid of the woman, but I honestly wasn't and wasn't going to pretend. I didn't move an inch. Neither did Abaddon. He was earning some points back.

"For the love of everything that fuckin' shouldn't be brought up," she groused. "NO, I didn't eat her. That was a one-time thing and it was fuckin' foul."

I nodded and put my hand over my heart to calm the racing. Pushing away the images of Candy Vargo chowing down on Pandora was harder, but I forced myself to do it. It was bad enough I'd already embarrassed myself in front of Abaddon and the powerful crowd. Throwing up would be too much to come back from.

"Define time-out," I said, holding my head high and standing my ground.

The Keeper of Fate's eyes narrowed. She clearly wasn't used to being called out. I didn't care. I was so done with this shit.

"You talkin' to me?" she demanded à la Robert DeNiro, but a lot scarier.

"Yeah, wise guy," I shot back. "I have a lot of stuff going on right now. If the cow-bitch is in time-out and I can go on with my life without looking over my shoulder all the time, I'd like to know. You feel me?"

"BALLS!" Candy Vargo shouted with a peal of delighted laughter. "Love it!"

I shook my head and grinned. She was nuts. "Thank you. Now answer me."

The batshit crazy woman snapped her fingers and conjured up a well-used leather recliner. She sat down, reclined and crossed her legs. "Pandora's in time-out for a decade."

My knees buckled with relief. Abaddon grabbed me before I hit the floor. My eyes filled with tears and I let them fall freely.

"My dad and brother are safe?"

She gave me a thumbs up.

"I'm safe?" I whispered.

Candy eyed me. "For now."

I grabbed her hand, yanked her out of the chair and hugged her hard. She didn't know what to do with my affection, but was a good sport. After patting me awkwardly on the back, she extricated herself from my embrace.

"I'll repay you," I promised. "What can I do for you?"

I noticed every Immortal in the room had a pained expression. Had I just committed a faux pas?

Candy Vargo scratched her head and considered my offer. "You still doin' that new TV show, Cecily Bloom?"

"I am," I replied warily.

"Great. I've always wanted to be on TV. Can you write a fuckin' pole dancer in?"

I now knew why everyone had winced. I was thinking more along the lines of a spa day, a lifetime supply of toothpicks or a really nice dinner out. Or even an offer to babysit her foster children.

My voice had left me. I couldn't get a word out. However, Cher could and did.

"I believe we can make that work, old lady," she assured Candy. "A bunch of forty-plus women trying out pole dancing to combat the middle-aged bulge could be comedy gold. We could show a few hot flashes and end the episode with boxed wine and nachos. We'll call the episode 'Hot Flash Dance!' Get it?"

I did. She might actually be onto something. Normally, I was terrified of my agent's artistic ideas, but this one was all kinds of brilliant.

"Done," I said, extending my hand to Candy. "We'll let you know when you have to be in LA for rehearsal." I was sure I'd live to regret it, but I would forever be in the woman's debt. An episode about hot flashes and pole dancing was a small price to pay.

Candy Vargo shook my hand then turned around and flipped off her group. "I'm gonna be on TV, motherfuckers!"

"Oh, hi, Gram," Daisy, the Angel of Mercy, said loudly.

"Where?" Candy clamped a hand over her mouth.

The Grim Reaper and his crew laughed. I didn't get the reference, but the sly smile on Daisy's face told me it was an inside joke at Candy Vargo's expense.

I shrugged as I looked around the room. "Are we done here?"

"We are not," Lilith said coolly.

"But we are," Gideon announced, crossing the room and standing in front of his sister. The formality between them was interesting and tense. "I still owe you, Lilith."

She waved her hand and gave him a tight smile. "You helped Cecily control her power. We're even."

Gideon nodded and walked back to Daisy and his group. "Cecily, we're blood. I shall make myself available to you and your mate for the rest of time. All you have to do is ask."

I tilted my head in confusion. "My mate?"

"Abaddon," Gideon clarified.

I shook my head. "Umm… not my mate," I said. "We haven't even gone on a date yet."

It was Gideon's turn to look confused. Daisy quickly pinched his arm. What was going on here?

"My apologies," Gideon said contritely. "I thought you were aware."

"Of?" I demanded.

"The compulsion," he replied.

Abaddon sucked in a sharp breath. Lilith shot her brother a furious glare. It made me feel itchy and insecure.

I'd heard the term. The definition basically meant being forced to do something against one's will. What the hell did that have to do with me? Or Abaddon?

"I'm not aware of any kind of compulsion," I said icily. "Would you care to explain?"

The Grim Reaper pressed his lips together then sighed. "I believe this is a discussion between you and Abaddon."

I glanced at the Demon in question. His eyes shot daggers at the Grim Reaper.

"My apologies. Until we meet again," Gideon said with a curt nod of his head.

In a blast of shimmering black mist, the Grim Reaper, the Angel of Mercy, Tim the Immortal Courier, the gal with the tattoos, the scary man with the icy blue eyes and Candy Vargo disappeared.

"Do we need to talk?" I asked Abaddon.

"I thought you were tired," he pointed out.

"Sleep can wait," I shot back. Something was off. There was no way I would sleep.

"We shall take our leave," Lilith said. "Sushi, may we stay the night?"

"Of course." Sushi clapped her hands. Five Succubi appeared. "Please show my guests to their suites."

Everyone left the private room except Abaddon and me. He was so stupidly beautiful. Nothing in my life had been easy in the romance department. My guess was that this wasn't going to be easy either. The thought made my stomach hurt.

Whatever. We hadn't even gone to dinner yet. If it was over before it began, so be it. My mind was on the same page, but my heart didn't want to listen.

"Start talking," I said, backing away from him.

He nodded his head. "As you wish."

CHAPTER FOURTEEN

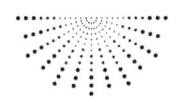

LILITH HAD SAID BEWARE OF WHAT YOU WISH FOR. SHE WAS WISE. Sometimes wishes were better left ungranted. The truth was often impossible and depressing to handle.

The conversation was not going what I would call great. It had been ongoing for twenty minutes and I was pretty sure I'd asked the same question in different ways twenty times hoping I'd finally get an answer.

It wasn't working out. Abaddon was the master of the vague reply.

"Do you actually own the movie studio?" I demanded, veering off the failed line of questioning I'd been pursuing. My list was long. I'd get back to the sickening part shortly.

Abaddon nodded. "I do."

"Where in the hell did you get the money to buy a studio?"

"Money is not and will never be an object," he replied. "I've been around a very long time, Cecily."

It was bizarre that I felt like we were contemporaries. We were not. The Demon was older than dirt.

"And the TV show?"

"*Ass The World Turns* will go on as planned," he told me. "It will be easier now that Pandora is out of the picture for a while. Although, we will not assume you're completely safe. In our world, no one is ever fully secure."

I didn't love the sound of that, but being cautious was smart. I was so tired, I felt drunk. It was time to get back to the part of the discussion that the Demon wanted to avoid. Fighting for my life was easier than getting an answer out of him. I was well aware I was most likely on the way to destroying my heart. I'd rather lop the head off of a flaming asshole than keep pressing for answers, but my gut told me to go for it. I was going to follow my gut even if it broke me. Candy Vargo thought I was a badass. Badasses didn't give up.

"I need the truth. All of it," I said, pacing the room and trying not to cry. The need to crawl out of my skin was strong. My brain raced and my heart pounded rapidly in my chest. Of course, this shitshow was my life… Why was I surprised? "I'm a *compulsion* for you?"

Abaddon sat down at one of the tables and pressed the bridge of his nose. "It's different for Demons."

"How?" I shouted. "How is being forced and having no choice in the matter different for Demons?"

I was so hurt and embarrassed I wanted to curl up into a ball and scream. I'd been cheated on. I'd been dumped. I'd had bad break ups and civil ones. I'd never experienced anything like this. Abaddon wasn't attracted to me. He wasn't falling for me. He was apparently programmed against his will to be with me.

"It just is, Cecily," he explained, frustrated. "What I feel for you is very real."

Why did he have to be so stupidly handsome? Just looking at him made my heart skip a beat. My heart was an idiot. I pointed at him and narrowed my eyes. "Because you have to," I accused. "Not because you want to."

"For us it's the same thing," he insisted.

"But not for me," I snapped. "I have free will. I choose who I love."

"And how's that worked out for you so far?" he asked with his eyes flashing.

Shit. Not great. "Just fine," I lied.

"And your marriage?" he pressed.

"Ended because I caught him in an orgy." I was way past being embarrassed. Slash broke our vows, not me. "I was young and stupid. I'm forty now and not as dumb. Plus, it's a good thing I used to be married to the jackass. He gave me the passes to get in and save your compulsed ass."

"And what do you have to do in return for the passes?" he ground out through clenched teeth.

He had some nerve… I reminded myself that his jealousy was fake. "I'm having dinner with Slash next week."

The Demon stood up, walked to the back wall and put his fist through it. I despised myself for thinking the move was hot. I didn't need therapy. I needed a lobotomy.

"You're *not* having dinner with him," he snapped.

I laughed. His eyes widened in shock. "You're not the boss of me, Dick. I'm the boss of me. Your people would have died if we'd stormed the building. You might have died. Dinner with an idiot is a small price to pay."

He didn't quite know what to do. He was clearly used to being obeyed. "Fine. I'll be joining you."

"Wrong," I shot back. "I'm a big girl. I don't need protection from a human."

"So be it," he finally conceded. Abaddon sighed, sat back down and tried another angle. "Have you ever thought that all of your relationships failed because you were waiting for me?"

"OH MY GOD," I screeched. "Your ego is enormous, Dick."

He grinned. "That's not all that's enormous, Cecily."

I wanted to punch him. However, I was terrified if I got too close, I'd jump him, get naked and shove my tongue down his throat while confirming the information he'd just thrown out there. My heart, my brain and my reproductive organs were at war.

"If you have to brag, you're compensating for something, *Dick*."

"Trust me, I'm not bragging." He squinted at me in annoyance. "So, we're back to calling me Dick?"

"If the shoe fits," I said with a shrug. I groaned and sat down at a table across the room from him. "I don't want this."

"Liar," he said. "You want me as badly as I want you."

"No, I'm not lying." All the cryptic words came flying back at me. I'd been too dumb to catch on. Cher had said it was impossible to screw up with Abaddon. My mother had said she understood my compulsion to save Abaddon even if I didn't. I'd like to think that I would have saved him because it was the right thing to do. Now I wasn't sure. Nothing made sense. Trusting my instincts was iffy. "I can't live like this."

"And how will you live out your life, Cecily?" he asked flatly.

I glared at him. "I'll live alone if I have to. I have friends and a family. I don't need a man. I have sex toys and self-respect. I will *never* want someone who is forced to want me."

"I'm trying to explain that this is how Demons work," he ground out. "I'm a Demon. I've waited for you since the beginning of time."

I rolled my eyes. "Bullshit. You were an asshole to me when we met."

He bit down on his lip. I was freaking jealous of his teeth. I wasn't sure if he was trying not to smile or not to yell at me. "I was surprised that it was you," he finally said.

"And clearly thrilled," I said with a humorless laugh. "Look, Dick, am I attracted to you? Sure. You're hot. Have I imagined naked, naughty stuff? You bet. However, I'm not going to be part of a couple that isn't organic. I want to fall in love and have someone fall in love with me. No compulsion involved."

"Beware what you wish for, Cecily," he said flatly. "Eternity is a very long time to be alone."

Again, I rolled my eyes. "I'm half-human. I won't be around for eternity and I'm pretty sure once Pandora is free of her time-out, I'll be a goner. That gives me a decade to kick off my shoes and have some fun. Yay me."

"Doubtful," he said.

"Which part?" I demanded.

"You'll be around for much longer than you'd like to believe," he informed me. "Your Goddess has kicked in."

"My what?"

He squinted at me. "You're glowing, Cecily. I know you're smart enough to know what that means."

I was going to have a chat with Lilith. I no longer trusted the devastatingly handsome Demon.

"I wish I'd never met any of you," I said hollowly.

Self-pity was unattractive, but I wanted to wallow in it. Life had been just fine before the secret of my heritage had been revealed. I was a mostly happy camper getting acting gigs and hanging out with my family and friends. My home was paid off. I adored my pickup truck. My collection of vibrators took the edge off of my needs. Watching cooking shows was fun. Maybe I'd take up knitting or crosswords.

Oh hell... I sounded like an over-the-hill spinster. Abaddon was correct. I was a liar. Lying was as unattractive as self-pity.

Honesty was overrated, but I was having an internal come to Jesus. I almost laughed that my mostly agnostic and Demon-self had just used a religious saying. Whatever. I did glance up to make sure a lightning bolt wasn't headed my way. At this point, I believed anything was possible.

My life had started when Abaddon had come crashing into it with his shitty attitude and rock-hard gorgeous body. I'd finally woken up. My possibilities had become endless. The Demon had made my dreams come true as an actress. Having my own show was my wildest wish come to life. And it was going to be such a damned good show.

All good things must come to an end. I wished it could be different.

The key word was *wish*.

Lilith had told me to be careful with my gift to cast spells. It could help as much as harm. Abaddon deserved to find love the natural way. I did too. It was stupefying to realize that my attraction to him wasn't real. As much as I wanted to ignore the cold hard truth, I couldn't. It was wrong. I was losing myself fast. Hanging onto my self-respect was about all I had left.

Yes, I was a Demon. There was no denying it. But that didn't mean that I would play by their rules. They were archaic and distorted.

I stared at the man who I thought was my happily ever after. My heart felt heavy in my chest.

"I'm so sorry, Abaddon," I whispered brokenly.

For what?" he asked warily.

I was about to do two things I'd never done. Poofing was one of them. It was probably stupid, but there was no way I was staying after the other part of my plan. Ophelia had explained that to poof, one simply had to visualize where they wanted to go. Easy enough. I wanted to go home.

"Sorry for this," I replied. "To whom it may concern, this spell is for the Demon Abaddon and the Demon Goddess Cecily."

Abaddon jumped to his feet. "Do *not* do this, Cecily."

Tears rolled down my cheeks. Abaddon looked heartbroken. It seemed so real, but I knew it wasn't. I was going to give him back his free will. Someday he would thank me.

"Love should be gentle. Love should be kind. It should come naturally, not by design. The compulsion deserves expulsion. May it darken no more. The world's a vast place. Who knows what's in store? I send out a plea to set both of us free. Right now, my heart breaks, but in time we will see. Thank you and have a good day."

It was the prettiest spell I'd cast so far… and the most heart shattering. I didn't look at Abaddon. I couldn't. It would be devastating to see that his feelings for me were dead.

Sadly, my heart didn't get the memo. The spell didn't work on me. The compulsion had apparently not been my cross to bear. I'd been falling for real. Too bad, so sad. It would have eventually destroyed me to know that he didn't love me because he wanted to.

Closing my eyes, I pictured my home. The tingling started in my chest then spread quickly to the rest of my body. As I vanished in a shimmering cloud of silver and red mist, I hugged my body tight. I'd get over him. I'd gotten over all the others. It would just take repeated reminders for the rest of my days that he'd been forced to love me.

I arrived in my living room in less time than it took to inhale. I felt shaky on my feet, and it was difficult to catch my breath. Dropping to the ground on all fours, I sucked in oxygen for all I was worth.

Cold and dead inside, the tears came unbidden. I cried so hard and for so long I lost track of time. As the sun rose, I crawled to my bedroom and buried myself under the covers.

Today was the first day of the rest of my life.

Without Abaddon.

Shit.

CHAPTER FIFTEEN

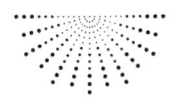

Prying my tear-swollen eyes open was difficult. When I'd gone to bed it had been light outside. It was dark now. For a brief moment, I didn't know where I was, what day it was or if I'd missed anything important. My reality came roaring back and made my head hurt.

"Crap," I muttered, sitting up and running my hands through my hair.

I didn't know where my phone was or if it had survived my poof. I was just glad I'd survived my poof. It was a hairy way to travel. My limbs still ached. However, my heart had my body beat.

The murmur of soft conversation coming from the living room forced me to get out of bed. Pressing my ear to the door, I listened. It was Man-mom, Sean, Uncle Joe, Cher, Ophelia and Fifi. The words were difficult to make out, but the tone was somber. It occurred to me that having Fifi in the same room as my brother might be an issue but I pushed the thought away. I trusted the Succubus. I knew in my gut she would never harm me or anyone who I loved.

"Shower," I said to my messy reflection in the full-length mirror on the back of the door. If I was going to face the people who I knew loved me because they chose to, I needed to wash away the hurt and pain. That was a tall order, but it was a start.

Grabbing a worn pair of jeans, my favorite sweatshirt, undies and tennis shoes, I tiptoed to the bathroom and quietly closed the door behind me. I shook my head and smiled when I saw the note taped to the mirror. My brother was the best kind of nuts. An array of edibles was in a coffee cup on the side of the sink. The note advised, to relax, eat the green one. To be giggle-high, eat the orange. To obliterate everything for a few hours, eat three of the red ones.

It was tempting, but I passed. Being stoned right now wasn't in my best interest. I had a lot to do and none of it was pleasant. Not only had I ended my false relationship, I was certain I'd ended the TV show as well. Abaddon wouldn't want to continue our collaboration now that he was free of me. Facing him and knowing that the spell didn't erase my feelings would be debilitating. It would kill me to watch him move on with someone else. Hopefully, he would steer clear of LA. I figured he would sell his house down the street and wash his hands of the woman he'd been compelled to love.

"Never dating again," I said, brushing my teeth. "Vibrators are far less complicated. The Succubi are onto something."

The thought of having to break the news to everyone that the show was dead made me weary. But I was the star, and the news was coming from me. There was no way that anyone I'd hired was going to find out the show was axed in the tabloids. I'd make sure the writers got paid and everyone else who'd put in work, even if it came from my own bank account.

Hell, there was so much buzz around the show, maybe

another studio would pick us up. Although, *Ass The World Turns* would forever remind me of Abaddon.

"You'll be fine, Cecily," I promised myself, tracing the outline of my lips and remembering his final kiss. "You're a badass. Badasses always survive."

I wasn't sure I believed my words, but if there was no goal, no goal could be accomplished. As the bathroom steamed up, I wrote the word badass and the phrase "let's get this party started" on the mirror. I felt calmer.

If I was able to pretend for long enough, I could make it come true. I wasn't one for method acting, but was willing to give it a shot.

After a quick shower, I twisted my wet hair into a messy knot and got dressed. I was clean. I smelled great. Forcing myself to smile at my reflection, I gave myself a weak thumbs up.

"Let's get this party started."

∼

"He did what?" I asked in horrified disbelief.

Fifi blew out a long breath. She, along with Cher and Ophelia, had driven my pickup home from Las Vegas. The Succubus had my back. Fifi was seated on the couch next to dead Uncle Joe, who was as naked as the day he was born. It was nice that she wasn't squeamish about Uncle Joe's nudity. It was terrific for my uncle to be with people who could see him. I wished that Sean and Man-mom could see him too, but that would mean they were Immortal. Being Immortal was turning out to be a curse.

"Please tell me I heard you wrong," I begged.

Fifi shook her head. "Right after you left, the Demon pulled the fire alarm so everyone cleared the Succubi club, then he blew up the building."

My hand flew to my mouth. "Did anyone get hurt?" I whispered through my fingers.

Ophelia shook her head. "Nope. But Abaddon is in a shitload of trouble with Lilith."

"Wow." It was the only word that came out. What in the world had Abaddon been thinking? He had his freedom. He should have been rejoicing. Demons were seriously screwed up.

Cher was sporting a lime-green power suit with purple eye shadow and royal blue lips. It was not her best look. "Would you like to talk about what happened with you and Abaddon?"

I shook my head. "No."

"Got it," she replied.

No one knew what to say. The silence was awkward. Uncle Joe offered to dance. Fifi gently suggested maybe it wasn't the right time.

"You okay, Cecily-boo?" Man-mom asked with concern etched on his lined and beautiful face.

I smiled at one of my favorite people in the world. Bill Jackson Bloom—BJ to his buddies—had singlehandedly raised me and Sean with a ton of love, cereal for dinner and regular therapy for all. My dad was a distracted mess of profound wisdom, horrible cooking skills, a time management deficit, and he gave the best bear hugs in the Universe.

"Getting there," I said.

He walked across the room and pulled me into his strong and loving arms. Sean joined him and Uncle Joe floated above us with his privates dangling. I giggled. It was appalling and somehow totally right. They made a Cecily sandwich. It was exactly what I needed. Being loved on by my brother, my uncle and my dad made my world a little more normal. Granted, having my uncle's balls almost touching my head was iffy, but the love outweighed the floating gonads.

Pressing his forehead to mine, Man-mom kissed my nose. "You met your mother?" he asked wistfully.

I nodded. I didn't want to talk about her. She was Lilith to me, not my mom. She would never be my mom. It was beyond clear that my dad still loved her, and I suspected she still loved him. Sharing my opinion on the matter might be painful, therefore, it was unnecessary. Upsetting my dad wasn't on the agenda. "I met her."

"And?" he pressed, curious.

"And that's it. I don't think I'll see her again," I told him. I kept my voice gentle even though it was difficult. Other than Ophelia, I was done with Demons. Staying away was smart. The pull into the sensual world of the Darkness was difficult to resist. Resisting Abaddon would be impossible. I didn't want that life. I had a damned good life right now filled with people I trusted and loved.

"I'm sorry, Cecily," he said. "I'd hoped it would be a wonderful experience."

I smiled and cupped his cheek in my hand. "You've given me forty years of wonderful experiences, Man-mom. I'm doing just fine."

"Did you partake in the gummies?" Sean asked with a lopsided grin.

I squinted at my brother and grinned back. He was a six-feet-tall, very handsome hot mess. I adored him. As strange as my only sibling was, he was also a world-renowned poet. He didn't make much of an income from his poetry, but he had legions of rabid and probably stoned fans. Sean made money by investing the income we'd made as kids. Because of his prowess in all things financial, we had an excellent retirement set up and absurdly healthy savings accounts.

Poetry was his passion. I couldn't make heads or tails of his non-linear verse, but he'd explained that one had to indulge in jazz cabbage—his favorite term for pot—to fully savor his creative genius. My guess was that meant there were tons of people in the world who were enjoying the Devil's Lettuce regularly—Sean's second-favorite term for Mary Jane. He'd also agreed to be the head writer on the TV show. He'd offered and I'd accepted. I'd been ready to beg my brilliant brother, but hadn't had to. Since *Ass The World Turns* was now in the crapper, I hoped he'd work on the next project with me.

"I didn't indulge. But I'll hang onto them for later," I told him.

"Good plan," he said with a wink as the front doorbell chimed.

As Sean walked toward the door, I sprinted past him and slammed my body against the wooden frame. My fingers began to spark. "Don't answer that," I hissed.

Fifi yanked a grenade from her pocket, and Ophelia whipped up a purple fire sword. Yes, Pandora was in time-out, but that didn't mean her flaming assholes weren't still after me. I had no clue if the barrier that protected my house and the street was still in effect. There was no way Man-mom and Sean would live through an attack.

"Dude," Sean said, putting his hands on my shoulders. "It's the pizza delivery guy. I ordered a bunch of pies."

Turning and peeking through the peephole, I expelled an enormous sigh of relief. On the other side of the door was a pimply teenager wearing a uniform and holding about ten pizzas.

Banging my head against the door, I wanted to disappear.

My fight-or-flight instinct was real. This was going to be a hard way to live. "My bad," I whispered, opening the door.

"I've got this," Sean said, gently moving me out of the way.

He paid the teen, took the pizzas and closed the door behind him.

I locked, chained and bolted it.

Everyone stared at me.

"Sorry," I said with a wince and a forced smile. "That was kind of overkill."

"Happens to everyone," Cher said, waving a yellow eye pencil at me. "No worries."

I squinted at her and smiled. She was nuts and I loved her. "I'd have to disagree. However, pizza sounds good."

After two slices of cheese, one slice of sausage, mushroom and jalapeno, and the crust that Sean didn't eat, I began to feel more like myself. "So, Cher, we have some tough phone calls to make."

My agent looked confused. "It's ten at night. Work can wait until tomorrow."

I shook my head. She didn't get it. There was no reason why she should get it. "There won't be any work tomorrow," I told her, feeling my stomach sink. It sucked to have lost my happily ever after both relationship-wise and career-wise.

"Bullshit," she said. "Just because you and Abaddon had a tiff and he blew up a building doesn't mean the show is dead. I have iron-fucking-clad contracts. I'll sue the shit out of everyone at the studio if they try to drop us."

"It wasn't just a tiff," I said, not wanting to explain, but realizing I had to tell them something.

All eyes were on me. I was full but ate another slice of cheese to buy some time. The minute it took for me to eat it didn't help much.

"I cast a spell and broke the compulsion," I said.

Ophelia paled and gasped. Cher's brows shot up to her hairline. Fifi seemed impressed. Man-mom, Sean and Uncle Joe looked confused.

"Compulsion?" Sean asked, handing me some more crust.

I half-wished he'd offered me three red gummies. Getting obliterated sounded pretty good right now.

"I'm going to explain, but I don't want any advice or pity, please." I glanced around. All nodded. Inhaling deeply, I dove in. "It's humiliating," I whispered, staring at my hands. "I was falling for Abaddon. For the first time in my life, I thought I was finally getting it right." I closed my eyes and pictured the devastated look on his face when he'd realized what I was doing. The pain I felt right now was visceral, but I knew I'd done the right thing. Sadly, my heart didn't believe me. "The joke is on me. I thought he was falling for me. He wasn't. He was under some kind of demonic compulsion to want me."

"A compulsion goes both ways," Ophelia said, then slapped her hand over her mouth when Fifi growled at her. "My bad. Won't happen again, bitch."

"Thank you, jackass," I said with a tired smile. "You're wrong. I wasn't under the compulsion. Maybe because I'm half-human. I was falling in love for real. The spell only worked on Abaddon."

"Well, that sucks all kinds of ass," Cher muttered, going into her bag and pulling out two six-packs of strawberry wine coolers.

I took one and continued. "So, it stands to reason he won't want to produce *Ass The World Turns*. He'd tried to play it off that the show was created so he could protect me, but he slipped up and said it was because it would make me happy. Trust me, Abaddon no longer wants to make me happy."

THE EDGE OF EVIL

Cher's royal-blue lips were now lined in white. "I'll sue."

"Nope," I said, holding up my hand. "I don't want that kind of press and it'll put a stink on the show. A tainted show is not what we want. It's a sure-fire fail."

Sean popped a gummy into his mouth and offered some to our guests. Only Fifi indulged. "Follow me," he said, thinking aloud.

"I will follow you to the ends of the earth, Sean Bloom," Fifi said, saluting my confused and slightly alarmed brother. "You have my word that I will never fornicate with you. I have far too much respect to suck the life force from your sexy and muscular frame."

Sean squinted at her for a long beat. "I'm going to go with a thank you on that," he told her.

My brother was very diplomatic and kind—and stoned. Fifi nodded enthusiastically and offered him a grenade. He passed.

"So," Sean continued. "I say instead of scrapping the show, we go after financing. I'm willing to put up a couple million. With the amount of good content needed for all the streaming services, I think we could find a home for the show quickly. The buzz is insane."

Fifi, clearly platonically besotted by Sean and absurdly loyal to me, chimed in. "I'll put up fifty million."

I choked on my pizza crust.

"I can put about ten million in," Ophelia offered. "I've won the lottery a few times."

"Did you cheat?" I asked, unable to truly absorb the numbers that were being tossed around so casually.

"No comment, bitch," she shot back with a naughty grin.

Cher pulled out a hot pink lip pencil and created eyebrows that defied nature. "Holy shit," she shouted. "I say we let the Demon can us and we move on. With that much moolah we can have our pick of streamers to call home. *And* we'd own the show. I'll negotiate a killer deal. Hell, we could start our own damned studio!"

I felt queasy, excited and terrified. "Hang on," I said, taking one of the mildest gummies from the pile Sean had placed on the coffee table and popping it into my mouth. "I'm not comfortable with you guys putting so much money in. It could bomb and everyone could lose their shirts. We need to go about it the normal way and look for studio backing."

Fifi raised her hand.

I acknowledged her with a nod.

"My liege, fifty million is nothing to me," the Succubus assured me. "I have billions in the Cayman Islands—maybe even trillions. I would be most honored to lose some cash to make my liege and her brilliant, muscular brother happy."

"Umm… that's really nice of you, Fifi, but I'm not sure," I told her.

"I sure as hell am sure," Cher announced. "Pretty sure I just had a freaking orgasm. Probably need to change my grundies. I say we put it to a vote. Majority wins."

Ignoring my agent's overshare, my mind raced with all the ways this could go horribly wrong. There were too many to count. So, I stopped counting. There was no way I could personally pay back all the money my friends wanted to invest. However, if they were willing to bet on me, I wasn't going to be the one who walked away unscathed if we failed.

Taking a deep breath and knowing that what I was about to say could bankrupt me, I put it out there before I could come to my senses and change my mind. "I can afford to lose five million. I'll add that to the kitty."

Man-mom grinned. "I have no plans to lose any money. I'll pony up ten million."

My mouth fell open. My dad would have to take out massive loans to invest like that.

"No can do, Man-mom," I said quickly.

He just smiled and pointed to my brother. Sean grinned.

"What don't I know?" I asked, eyeing both of them suspiciously.

"Shall I?" Sean asked Man-mom.

"Be my guest," he replied, looking at my sibling with love and pride.

Sean popped another gummy into his mouth and rubbed his hands together with glee. "Bill's multimedia art business with the Underworld theme has been rocking for the past five years. After taxes last year, the talented old man pulled down twenty-five million. And that was down from the thirty million from the year before. Bill's a real badass with the Hades subject matter. I did a little investing for him here and there and doubled his money. Man-mom is set for several lifetimes, even with the millions upon millions he donated to charity. Total badass."

I was pretty sure my mouth had just gotten stuck in a permanent and unattractive O. With or without the money, my dad was a badass. However, he'd just reached the next level.

"I'm in the wrong fucking business," Cher muttered with a chuckle, adding up the numbers. "Sean, you wanna start investing for me?"

"It would be my pleasure, Cher," he replied.

Still in shock, I sat down next to Uncle Joe and used my hands to physically close my mouth. I hadn't looked at my investments in a long while. I let Sean handle that. "Can I afford to put in more than five mil?"

Sean nodded. "Yep."

"How much more?"

My brother pulled his laptop out of his man-purse and brought up my accounts. I walked across the room and looked over his shoulder. I almost puked. The numbers had so many zeros I couldn't get my brain to comprehend.

"Can half of that go to charity?" I whispered as I gripped the back of the chair in disbelief.

Sean ran some numbers. "How about ten million to charity and you invest ten mil in the show? That'll still leave you more than financially secure."

I sank to the floor so slowly it looked like a bit in a comedy gag. "That'll work."

"We have more than we need," Cher sang. "I say we shoot the pilot without any studio backing then let them fight over who gets it."

"You're banking that everyone's going to want it," I said, crawling over to the couch on my hands and knees.

"I'm a gambling sort of gal," Cher announced. "And I'm feelin' real lucky."

Sean walked over, helped me to my feet, then gently sat me down on the couch next to Uncle Joe. He squatted down in front of me. "The show is a winner, Cecily," he said. "The writing, if I may brag for a moment… is flat-out genius. The concept that *you* came up with is comedy gold. You've gathered the best of the best with the cast, staff and crew. If we stay humble and work harder than we've ever worked, we can't lose."

His words were nice, but in showbiz there was always a way to lose.

I needed something to do. Pouring my passion into something I loved would help me obliterate Abaddon from my head and heart.

Who was I kidding? That would take time and time

marched on slowly. It was impossible to make it move at a faster pace. However, being busy and productive was a solid plan. Plus, after I'd seen my financials, I realized I could pay everyone back if we were a bust.

I smiled. Looking around the room, I felt blessed beyond belief that I was loved by choice. "I say we get this party started."

Everyone whooped and cheered.

"First we get our asses canned by Abaddon, then we get to the real work," Cher announced.

My heart seemed to get stuck in my throat. "You think he'll be at the studio tomorrow?"

Ophelia shook her head. "Highly doubtful. Like I said, his ass is in some big trouble for blowing up Sushi's club."

"Doesn't matter," Cher said, pulling a bottle of champagne from her bottomless bag. "Demons—even those who are in the shithouse with their Goddess—never let their business go. My guess is that someone else will be there to fire us tomorrow."

As if on cue, her phone buzzed. Cher looked at it and smiled. "Studio just called a meeting with Cecily and me at 10 AM sharp tomorrow morning! Kids, we're gettin' FIRED!"

Again, all my buddies cheered. Uncle Joe did a dance and encouraged everyone to join. It was nuts. Ophelia put on Donna Summer's greatest hits per Uncle Joe's request and the party truly started. I tried to catch the excitement bug, but couldn't. As happy as I was that the show would go on, I'd left most of my heart with the Demon who'd just caused massive property damage. Reminding myself he didn't want me anymore helped a little. The saddest part of the story was that I wanted him more than ever.

When was I going to learn that a man would not be my happily ever after? At forty fabulous years old, I was a strong and independent woman. I had a ridiculously healthy bank account thanks to my brother. I had a family who adored me and dear friends who had my back in a big way. Needing a man to complete me was bullshit. My thoughts were on point. Now I just needed to convince myself to believe them.

Good luck to me.

CHAPTER SIXTEEN

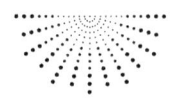

The day dawned bright, sunny and cloudless—very typically LA. My mood was anything but. At six in the morning my phone started buzzing repeatedly. Stupidly, I thought it might be Abaddon telling me he loved me even without the compulsion.

It was not Abaddon.

It was Slash.

My ex was texting about our dinner date. He'd left paragraphs about how the concert had been canceled and how sad his cock was that he'd missed me. The amount of eye rolling I'd done as I read was enough to make my eyeballs get stuck in the back of my head.

Slash the Rash also texted that he and the band had clearly done too many drugs over the years and had hallucinated at the venue. He'd explained that all sorts of crazy shit had gone down. He told me that he'd now sworn off drugs, alcohol, bimbos and orgies, and was hoping I'd give him and his pecker another chance. He even offered not to go Dutch this evening.

Our dinner was at 8 PM at the sushi place in Malibu where we'd gone on our first date.

The irony that I was going to eat sushi on a date from hell after Abaddon had just detonated Sushi's club didn't escape me.

I came seriously close to deleting the entire text, but didn't. I'd made a promise and I would keep it. After tonight, Slash Gordon would know very clearly that he and his pecker had no chance with me. Ever. The other reason I didn't bag was because the passes had helped us save Abaddon. It was a relief to know that I hadn't been under a compulsion to rescue the Demon. It had been the right thing to do. It had been what I'd wanted to do. Honestly, I'd done it because I was falling in love with him. Sadly, I'd do it again even though he didn't love me anymore.

Why?

Because I was an idiot and a glutton for punishment.

After trying to compose a text back to Slash, I gave up and sent a thumbs up emoji. My fingers wanted to tell him his pecker wasn't impressive and that he was a pig. That was mean. Slash was a dumbass, but he wasn't evil—just stupid. I would pay my debt and move on.

~

"You look gorgeous," Jenni said, admiring her handiwork.

I smiled at one of my besties. Jenni had been on *Camp Bite* with Sean and me back in the day. She'd played our bubbly human cohort who found all the clues for our undead missions. Jenni was ten years older and a whole lot smarter in the scheme of life. After the show ended, she'd left the acting game, gone to cosmetology school and was now a top-notch makeup artist in the biz. She was small in stature, sexily plump with an insanely cool silver streak in the front of her wild red hair. I'd hired her to be the head of hair and makeup on *Ass The World Turns*.

"Thanks to you," I told her, examining my sleek and sophisticated look in the mirror she'd handed me.

While she did my hair and makeup, I'd gotten Jenni up to speed on the fate of the show as much as I could while leaving out all the supernatural stuff. I'd boiled it down to a disastrous and bridge-burning fight with Abaddon. She had the same idea as Cher to sue the shit out of the studio, but changed her tune when she learned of the new financing. My delightful buddy even offered to invest 100K.

I was humbled by her belief in me and the project, but I didn't want Jenni to lose a cent and tried to pass. Jenni was hearing none of it. She wanted in on the ground floor of what was promising to be the hit of the decade.

From her mouth to God's ears. Although, I wasn't sure a Demon could legally use that phrase…

Fifi and Ophelia had taken to Jenni immediately and stood in line to be gussied up as well. Jenni was a great sport and made the gorgeous gals look even more stunning than they already did. She'd even had a go at Cher. My agent was concerned that she looked a little pale, but Sean convinced her she looked hot. Cher giggled like a schoolgirl and didn't even go for a lip pencil.

The only people actually going to the meeting were Cher and me. We'd dressed for success, or in our case, a firing. Cher was wearing a black Prada power suit that was only one size too small and heels that gave her a good four inches. I chose red—a red fitted Chanel dress and black Jimmy Choo stilettos. The raw silk sleeveless number came just above my knee with a square neckline that displayed my collarbone. It was classic and hugged my body like a very expensive glove, showing off all my best assets. Man-mom, Uncle Joe and Sean had heartily approved.

"Dude," Jenni said, drooling over my dress. "Did you get that on sale?"

Jenni was very aware that I hated paying full price. I was an outlet and sale rack kind of gal. There was no way I could explain that Cher had whipped up the outfit with a snap of her fingers.

"Clearance, basically free," I told her, crossing my fingers behind my back.

Cher chuckled. A horrible thought occurred to me. Where were these clothes actually coming from? Was she stealing them? Crap. We were going to have to have a discussion. Pilfering designer duds wasn't going to work for me.

"Those studio assholes are gonna rue the day they fired you," Jenni said, packing up her potions and brushes then giving me a hug. "I'm going to get over to the lot and clear out all my stuff just in case we get locked out after the meeting."

"Good thinking," Cher said, handing Jenni a set of keys. "Can you get anything Sushi might have left at the studio? She's got a little emergency on her hands this morning."

Jenni paled. "Did her boob job get infected?"

Cher was speechless. Hard to do. Fifi jumped right in.

"No, her bosom is fine. Sushi had to go to Vegas to deal with a small fire in a costume warehouse she owns. Looks like it will be fine, but she needs to take inventory," Fifi lied smoothly.

"Oh gosh, that sucks," Jenni said. "Tell her that I can be in Vegas in a few hours if she needs help."

Fifi already liked Jenni. She now loved her. "You are a fabulous human and I shall relay the message to Sushi."

Jenni blinked at the strange compliment, but to her credit, went with it.

Of course, then Fifi added, "Because of your kindness, I'll help you clear out your supplies. If anyone tries to stop us, I will kill them."

I glared at Fifi. She winced.

"I was joking, of course!" the Succubus yelled. "I'll just maim them."

It was my turn to wince. Jenni wasn't sure what was going on. When Ophelia jumped into the conversation, I held my breath in terror.

"I'll come too," she announced, giving Fifi a look that would wither a lesser being. "It'll go faster with three. Fifi's a real joker. She watches too many action flicks."

"Correct," Fifi agreed quickly. "I find Keanu Reeves alluring, which is why I will never bang him."

"Mmkay," Jenni said with a laugh. "Good to know. We ready to boogie?"

"We're going to dance?" Fifi asked, perplexed.

"Stop talking." Ophelia gave the Succubus an enormous eye roll. "It's not going well. In my estimation you've already shoved your foot so far down your throat, it's close to coming out of your ass."

Fifi looked over her shoulder at her backside.

Jenni laughed harder. "Oh my God. You two should do a comedy act. You're hilarious!"

"Really?" Ophelia asked, delighted. "Thank you!"

Fifi was just confused. Ophelia pushed her out of the front door as Jenni grabbed her bags. "They have to be actresses."

"That they are," Cher said with a wink. "Batshit crazy ones, but good girls."

"Trust me," Jenni said with a smile as she walked towards the front door. "I've dealt with far crazier. We'll be just fine."

As Jenni closed the door behind her, I had a semi panic attack. "Do you think Fifi will actually maim people?"

"Hard to say, but hopefully not," Cher said, glancing over at Uncle Joe.

Uncle Joe was doing yoga. Naked. It wasn't something I wanted to look at, but my agent didn't seem to take issue with his bouncing nuts.

"Joe, can you go with them? Jenni can't see or hear you. You can help keep the gals in line," Cher suggested.

"Wonderful!" Uncle Joe said, untwisting himself from his pose. "I adore being useful."

With his balls flopping in the wind, my beloved uncle flew through the wall of my house and into Jenni's SUV. I peeked out of the window. Neither Fifi nor Ophelia showed surprise. Of course, Jenni had no clue there was a naked dead man sitting next to her. I pressed the bridge of my nose and laughed. Could my life get any stranger?

I hoped not.

"You ready to get fired?" Cher asked with a grin.

"Bring it on," I replied. "Let's get this shitshow started."

"It's party," she corrected me, picking up her bottomless purse and slinging it over her shoulder.

"Remains to be seen," I said.

~

Just like the last time, Cher and I were escorted directly into the office that had once been Abaddon's.

THE EDGE OF EVIL

Just like the last time, there was no one there but us.

The room was huge and imposing. Money oozed from every pore of the over-the-top office. The couches were a buttery brown leather. The walls were a deep shade of green and tasteful art hung on three of them. The fourth wall was floor-to-ceiling windows that had an excellent view of the Hollywood Sign. Hardwood floors, so shiny they looked wet, were partially covered with gorgeous rugs in muted shades of cream and brown. The furniture was heavy and ornate. Everything except the walls was either black, brown or beige. It was easy to feel small and inconsequential in the room, which was probably the point.

The last time I'd been here, Abaddon had saved my life from being destroyed by Pandora's flaming assholes. I'd repaid the favor. We were even. Part of me hoped that Abaddon was about to walk through the door. A bigger part of me was relieved that he wouldn't. I wondered how much trouble he was in for blowing up the Succubi club. Lilith could be terrifying when pissed.

"Did you bring the contracts?" I asked, pacing back and forth.

Cher reached into her bag and pulled them out. "Yep. Worthless pieces of paper."

I nodded. Something felt incredibly off but I couldn't put my finger on it. After about twenty minutes of waiting, I was ready to leave.

"This is just rude," I said, running my hands through my hair.

"Demons," she said. "Rude to the core except for you and Ophelia."

I almost laughed. "Ophelia's kind of iffy."

"We're working on it," she replied with a wink. "I'll get that gal in shape to be the next Vanna White if it kills me."

"I hope it doesn't," I told her.

Cher cackled. "I'm hard to kill. Takes some doing to be around for twelve million years."

It still floored me that she was that old. "What's your real name?"

She scrunched her nose. "Engelbertina," she said with a groan. "Sounds like Engelbert Humperdinck, for the love of everything just wrong. Not that I'd kick the man out of my bed for eating crackers. He's a fine specimen of manhood, but the name sucks. It's German in origin, means bright Angel."

I grinned. "I like it."

She gave me the stink eye. I giggled.

"If you call me by that name, I'll send you out on cadaver roles."

"Got it. Won't use the name."

And I wouldn't. However, it was excellent blackmail material if I ever needed it.

"Do you think one of the Demons we met in Vegas will show up to fire us?" Cher asked, pulling out a lip pencil and going to town.

I didn't stop her. It was clearly her way of coping with stress. At least it was red.

I shrugged. "No clue. Although, it would be nice to see Dagon again. He was the friendliest. Being fired by him wouldn't be too bad."

I secretly wished it would be Abaddon. I wanted to see that he was okay and not in some kind of awful time-out like Pandora.

Beware of what you wish for. It rarely turns out the way you hope.

Three Demons strode into the office and straight to the desk. None made eye contact until they'd settled themselves. My stomach sunk to my toes and I wanted to run. I didn't run. Instead, I reached into my Chanel clutch and grabbed the box of toothpicks Candy Vargo had given me. I didn't put one into my mouth, but the feeling of the box under my fingertips reminded me that I was a badass. I didn't feel like a badass, but I was excellent at pretending.

Abaddon glared at me from behind the massive desk. He was furious and beautiful. My heart pounded in my chest and I sucked back the desire to cry. Dagon stood behind him to his left. Shiva, wearing a smug expression of victory, stood behind him to his right. When she placed her hand on his shoulder, it took everything I had not to whip up a purple fire sword and lop her head off.

The silence was deafening. I refused to speak first. They'd called the meeting. Not us.

Cher didn't have a problem talking. It was one of her superpowers.

"So, we're fired," she said with a tight-lipped smile. "I won't sue. I should, but I won't. We don't want to work with you assholes any more than you want to work with us."

Abaddon's brows shot up in surprise, but he didn't counter or correct my agent. Cher pulled out a sheaf of papers that I hadn't seen and slapped them down on the desk.

"Since we've been canned, I want the rights for the show signed back over. If you don't, I will sue you and I will own you. It's customary to pay the writers and crew who have already put in time, but we'll let that slide. All we want is ownership of our artistic material."

"No," Abaddon said in an icy-cold tone to Cher while staring at me. "No deal. I own the show. I'm keeping it."

I hadn't seen this coming, but I should have. He despised me and wanted me to suffer. His asshole status had just reached new heights. A whole hell of a lot of jobs were on the line. By punishing me, he was hurting others. This was bullshit.

"Well, Dick, you've reached a new low," I pointed out flatly.

Shiva growled. I rolled my eyes.

"Zip it," I ground out through clenched teeth. "You're already on thin ice with me, Sheba. Do not make me do something that you'll regret."

"It's Shiva," she hissed.

"Whatever," I shot back. "Dick's a big boy and can fight his own battles. Right, Dick?"

Abaddon's eyes narrowed. "Do you derive pleasure from getting everyone's names wrong?"

"Tons," I replied with a smile that didn't reach my eyes. My heart was shredding itself in my chest, but that was my business, not anyone else's. "There's no good reason other than spite to hold onto a show you have no plans to shoot."

"Spite is a delightful thing," he said with a shrug.

Our stare down was short but loaded. His expression was full of loathing. I kept mine neutral, which seemed to piss him off even more.

"How much?" I demanded.

"How much what?" he asked.

"How much do you want for the artistic rights?" I clarified.

He laughed. I flipped him off. I wasn't sure, but I thought Dagon's lip quirked up. I honestly liked him, but he was playing for the other team now. Shiva leaned into Abaddon and whispered in his ear. He pushed her away. Her embarrassment was incredibly enjoyable to watch. She couldn't bring herself to look at me. However, in the brief moment our eyes met, I winked at her. I was very aware it was killing her not to kill me. Too bad, so sad.

Cher started to hyperventilate. I'd come prepared. Reaching into my clutch, I pulled out a paper bag and handed it to her. She sucked on it like it was a lifeline.

"I'm not joking, Dick. How much do you want?"

Abaddon picked up the papers Cher had put on his desk and scanned them. His gaze met mine as he tore them in half. "You don't have enough money to buy back the rights."

"You'd be surprised at how much money I have."

"No, I wouldn't. I know exactly how much money you have," he replied.

My fury was real. My fingertips began to spark and I wanted to dive over the desk and rearrange his stupidly handsome face. If he had access to my bank accounts, what else did he have access to in my life?

"What are you?" I asked. "A stalker?"

"Something like that," he replied smoothly.

I shook my head and tried to shake off my ire. It wasn't working. "So, that's it? We're fired and you're keeping the show?"

Abaddon stood up and walked around his desk. The move was as sexy as it was terrifying. Terrifying because there was a damned good chance that I would jump him like a cat in heat. That would be beyond humiliating. I backed away as he continued to move closer. Biting down on my lips, I steeled myself, stopped and held my ground. He hated me. I loved him. It was a shitty fact of life. While I was eighty-five percent sure he wasn't going to kill me, the fifteen percent of being unsure was scary.

"Who said you were fired, Cecily?" he inquired, invading my personal space.

Shit. He had me there. "Umm… I thought it was a given."

"Don't think," he shot back. "It doesn't seem to be your forte."

"You're a dick, Dick."

His delicious scent was making me woozy. The need to touch him was almost debilitating. I gripped the toothpicks for all I was worth. My reproductive parts were going haywire. I needed to get the hell out of here.

"Possibly," he agreed. "You're not fired. You're doing the show."

My mouth moved before my brain had a chance to review the contents. "Bullshit. I'll quit."

Cher was about to blow a hole in the bag.

Abaddon smiled. It was mean. "I'll sue you for all you're worth, Cecily. And remember… I know exactly what you're worth."

Closing my eyes, I tried to figure out what to do. If he wouldn't sell or give us back the rights, there was no show. If I quit, I knew he'd destroy me financially and enjoy it. So many jobs were on the line. The show was my dream come true and Dick was turning it into a nightmare. It was my once-in-a-lifetime chance. He knew it and I knew it. The Demon had me by the balls and was twisting hard.

"We'll do the show," I finally said in a voice that should have frozen him into a block of ice.

He simply raised a brow.

"We will?" Cher choked out.

"We will," I told her then turned my attention back to the asshole who wanted to ruin me. "But the terms are unsatisfactory. I don't want a rush job. I want time. And I don't want you anywhere near the process."

The Demon took another step towards me. Our bodies were almost touching and I could feel the heat coming from his huge frame. It was as if he knew I still loved him and he wanted to torture me. It was working. "You can have your time, Cecily. However, I will be there *every* step of the way. Non-negotiable."

I swallowed all the foul things I wanted to say. Maybe this was exactly what I needed. If he was a viper all the time it would kill my feelings for him. When I was away from the Demon, I kept mulling over all of the good. It was no longer good and never would be. The harsh reality of his viciousness was the reality check I needed. Nothing killed love more than hatred. And he definitely hated me. Not to mention, he obviously had Shiva to take to his bed.

"As you wish," I replied emotionlessly.

"I wish," he replied coolly.

I smiled. It was forced. "Beware of what you wish for, Abaddon. It never turns out like you want it to."

He let out an irritated huff. "You think?" I held his gaze until he turned his back on me and walked over to the window.

I helped Cher to her feet and cleared my throat. "We're taking the rest of the week off," I announced in a brook-no-bullshit tone. "We'll send over paperwork with the new timeline. We should be up and running by January."

No one said a word. I nodded politely to Dagon and ignored the seething Shiva. She was a bitch, and not the good kind like Ophelia.

Without another word, I led Cher out of the office. It wasn't until we got into my pickup truck that either of us spoke a word.

"We're fucked," she said, still clutching the paper bag.

"Totally," I agreed, turning on the ignition and pulling out of the parking lot.

"Although, I've been way more fucked than this," Cher confided. "This is bad but not like being burned at the stake bad. If you can keep yourself from castrating the son of a bitch, I think we can do it."

I glanced over at her and shook my head. "I've never castrated anyone in my life."

"There's a first time for everything," she replied. "As the saying goes, keep your friends close and your enemies closer."

"Is that our new motto?" I asked, stopping at a red light and resting my forehead on the steering wheel.

"Nah," she said, handing me a blue eye pencil. "It's still let's get this party started. But we'll keep the other one on standby."

When you can't beat them, join them. I lined my lips in blue and put a toothpick into my mouth. "I can do this."

"Darn tootin'," Cher said. "You can fly, Cecily Bloom. I have proof."

I refrained from telling her that what goes up must come down. It was cliché but it was also true. I had every intention to fly. I'd just have to be wary of Abaddon trying to shoot me out of the sky.

While I didn't necessarily believe in fate, maybe this was happening for a reason. None of my friends or family would have to risk any money. Abaddon's wrath would kill my love. And I was going to kick ass on *Ass The World Turns*.

I was a badass and I was about to prove it… even if it hurt.

CHAPTER SEVENTEEN

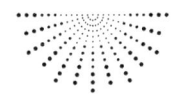

"Carbs," I muttered as I flopped down on the couch and contemplated my next move. The disastrous possibilities were endless. "Carbs are so delicious."

When I'd gotten back to the house after the shitshow with Abaddon, I changed into jeans and a t-shirt and grabbed the leftover pizza from last night. The meeting had taken it out of me. I left the blue eye pencil on my lips. Cher was my hero with Candy Vargo coming in a close second. I would have honored her as well, but eating cold pizza with a toothpick in my mouth wasn't happening. Enough people wanted me dead. I refused to help them out by choking on a piece of wood.

Seeing Abaddon had sucked. My body's reaction to him was obscene. The curve balls that had been thrown were unnerving. Observing Shiva touch him was infuriating. I was wildly proud of my self-control. The temptation to remove her head had been strong.

My gut said Abaddon would do everything in his power to make me miserable. Fine. The Demon could mess with me all he wanted. I was a big girl. What I had no intention of doing was failing. No matter how badly he treated me, I would protect the show for all I was worth... which was apparently a lot.

After giving me the blue eye pencil to keep, Cher had gone to her office to draw up the paperwork for a new timeline that made sense. Rushing the show was no longer happening. That was an enormous relief. What I needed right now was a little me-time to decompress. Since I wasn't alone, decompression was off the table.

"Oh! Cecily, darling! I feel like I've finally earned the title of Captain Nude-man," Uncle Joe squealed as he zipped all over the living room with his privates dangling while talking a mile a minute. "It was thrilling!"

Uncle Joe was all atwitter. He'd successfully helped divert a bloodbath at the studio. Security had tried to stop Jenni from taking her belongings. They'd confiscated her personal items and pulled out handcuffs. Fifi lost her debatably sane mind and almost decapitated the guards. I needed to ask Sushi if Succubi were forbidden from harming humans like Demons were. Although, to be fair, I didn't have proof that the security guards were human. As Ophelia had pointed out on our drive to Vegas, LA was filled with Demons and jerks.

"I've never blinded anyone with my balls!" Uncle Joe sang, doing flips in the air.

My beloved uncle's method of diversion had been to momentarily blind Fifi with his gonads. He'd wrapped his legs around her head like a blindfold of wrinkled balls to stop her from killing the security detail. I'd almost choked on my own spit as he graphically described the situation. Of course, he was transparent, but testicles in the face—even ghostly ones—had to be shocking.

While Fifi had an eyeful of nuts, Ophelia had covertly

shoved the Succubus into the guards and knocked her feet out from underneath her. The Demon freaked out, and at the top of her lungs accused the security officers of purposely tripping and maiming a helpless woman. When they'd tried to deny Ophelia's story, she whipped out her cellphone and began recording their every move while narrating her version of the events. Fifi caught on fast and began sobbing and moaning like she was dying. She'd even slammed her head down on one of the officer's boots and broke her nose. Ophelia accused the guard of kicking Fifi and said she had filmed proof. There was blood everywhere. When Ophelia began taking photos of their credentials covered in Fifi's spurting blood and talking about her hard-ass lawyers, the security crew backed off… and ran away.

My friends left the building with all of Jenni's supplies. The guards would probably need therapy. Jenni was traumatized until Fifi lied and told her it was all a hoax. The Succubi explained she carries fake blood bags because she moonlights as a stunt woman. The fact that she healed up immediately made Jenni believe the outlandish fib.

The entire story gave me gas. Although, I made a mental note to get the names of the security guards who'd harassed my people. They would be banned from coming anywhere near my set or anyone working on the show.

To celebrate not getting arrested, the gals went shopping on Fifi's black AMEX card. Uncle Joe had come home to tell me the story. Cher had promised to text the news on the lack of getting fired to everyone. That was good. I didn't have the energy.

"That's really something," I told Uncle Joe, trying to show some enthusiasm. The exhaustion was real. I would most likely fall asleep over raw fish on my dinner date tonight with Slash.

"Sweetie," Uncle Joe said, floating down and seating himself next to me on the couch. "I'm so sorry. All I've been doing is bragging on my stellar ball work. Tell me about getting fired. Was it wonderful?"

He put his ghostly arms around me. They went right through me, but it was the thought that counted.

"Not fired," I said morosely with a mouthful of pizza.

"Oh my," Uncle Joe said, fanning himself. "Is that good or bad?"

I finished chewing and swallowed. "Neither. It is what it is. Abaddon was his usual dickish self and refused to give back or sell us the artistic rights. Said he's still producing it. He was awful. The man despises me and wants to see me go belly up. The asshole will have to wait a very long time."

"Interesting. Very interesting," my uncle said, scratching his now infamous balls.

I side-eyed him. "What's very interesting?"

"Would you like to do yoga with me?" he inquired. "I find that deep conversation goes well with stretching the body. It centers the mind."

Yoga was the last thing I wanted to do, but disappointing the adorable man wasn't on the to-do list. "Sure," I said, getting down on the floor. "You lead. I'll follow."

For fifteen silent minutes, I followed my uncle's moves while avoiding looking at his privates. It was difficult but doable. Lo and behold, he was correct. I felt more centered and less stressed than I had in a while.

Uncle Joe sat crisscross applesauce and smiled at me lovingly. "When it rains look for rainbows. When it's dark look for fireflies. Always find the magic."

I smiled back. His words were nice, but didn't mean

anything to me. "What did you mean when you said very interesting?"

His smile grew wider. "It's okay to cry a river, beautiful child. Just make sure you build a bridge so you can get over it."

"I'm trying," I told him as my eyes welled up.

"I know, my sweet. And you're doing a stellar job," he said. "There's a very thin line between love and hate."

I inhaled slowly and exhaled loudly. "Not sure where you're going with this, but the direction seems a little iffy."

"I find it very interesting how angry Abaddon is with you. Do you know why?"

I shrugged. "Because he's a dick."

"Quite possible," he agreed. "But it doesn't make sense. You gave him his freedom. His behavior doesn't add up."

"Demons are batshit crazy," I told him, then laughed. "I suppose that makes me insane as well."

"In only the best way," he assured me. "I trust no one who isn't a little off their rocker. Being slightly gonzo is a mark of a fascinating person with artistic flair."

He'd just described himself, Sean, Man-mom and me, perfectly. We were a family of nuts… and his were exposed for the world to see.

"Abaddon is just an angry man," I said. "And he's no longer my problem."

Uncle Joe was quiet for a long beat. "But you still love him, my dear."

I stood up and out of habit extended my hand to help my uncle to his feet. He giggled as his hand went through mine. Again, it was the thought that counted.

"Yep, I love him, but at the rate he's going right now, I should be able to hate him by next week."

"Good girl!" Uncle Joe said. "Both you and your father

struck out in the loving a Demon department. Breaks my heart. You and Bill are such glorious people with so much to give. How about next time you fall in love, you go for a vampire? You were such an adorable vampire on *Camp Bite!*"

My laugh was loud. It felt cathartic. "I'll keep the suggestion in mind. Although, I'm ninety-nine percent sure they don't exist."

"Don't be hasty, Cecily-boo," he said, using the nickname that Man-mom had given me. "Until recently we didn't know about Demons, Angels and Succubi. Maybe the undead are living and sparkling among us as well."

I seriously hoped not. Demons, Angels, Succubi and regular Immortals were about all I could handle.

∼

"DO YOU WANT ME TO GO AND SIT AT THE BAR?" SEAN ASKED AS he made grilled cheese for Man-mom and himself in my kitchen. Their house was uninhabitable for the evening since Man-mom had lacquered his latest masterpiece—a life-sized painting of hellhounds frolicking with Bigfoot in a meadow of thorny roses. I had no idea if it was a commission or just a flight of bizarre fancy. "If Slash pulls anything shitty, I'll take care of him for you, sis."

I smiled at my goofy brother. He might be younger, but his protection gene was showing. He'd been concerned when I'd gone over the results of the meeting with Abaddon, but was convinced we could still make it work even with a pissy asshole producer. Man-mom was torn. He'd known Abaddon for much longer than I had and had considered him a friend. He was both saddened and angry at the colors the Demon had shown.

Honestly, it was a good thing Abaddon had shown his ass. I was leaning more into the idea of fate with each passing day. The Demon had arrived when I'd needed him. He'd forced me to accept who I was, taught me to fight and saved my life. He'd called on my uncle Grim Reaper to help me control my power. In return, I'd used that power to rescue him and repay him for what he'd done.

Pandora was in time-out thanks to the toothpick-loving Candy Vargo. I'd even been able to fulfill my lifelong dream of meeting the woman who'd given birth to me. I could check that off and move on. A relationship with Lilith wasn't in the cards. It was entirely too complicated. She'd made a choice when I was born, and she and I both had to live with it.

Most importantly, my dad and brother were safe. My feelings for Abaddon would fade with time. My love for Sean and Man-mom never would.

"Trust me, I can handle Slash."

"I'm a phone call away," Sean said, kissing my nose.

"And I'll call if I need backup," I promised.

The sushi restaurant in Malibu was impossible to get reservations at unless you were somebody or knew somebody. For me, the place was a huge eye roll, but I was paying a debt and the food was good. I'd dressed with care, making sure my outfit wasn't too revealing. I didn't need Slash getting any ideas or ogling my girls.

"You look lovely," Man-mom said with a nod of approval and a warm smile.

My dad had paint in his hair and all over his clothes. The lines around his eyes were from laughing and his smile made me feel loved. Granted, our upbringing had been non-traditional, but I wouldn't trade it.

"Thank you, Bill," I said, doing a twirl.

My sundress was modest by LA standards, but it was pretty and comfortable. I'd gotten the Alice and Olivia number on sale last year and had only worn it a few times. I'd paired it with gold flats and simple gold jewelry. My hair was twisted up into a knot and I'd gone with very little makeup with no blue lipliner. This wasn't a real date. It was a payment for a favor.

"I won't be out late," I told my dad, giving him a kiss on the cheek then grabbing my purse and a light jacket.

Sean expertly flipped the grilled cheese and waved. "Remember, I'm just a phone call away."

I waved back and walked out the front door. Glancing down the street, I zoned in on Abaddon's house. The crazy Demon had bought a house on my street. I'd half expected to see a for sale sign in the yard. The house was dark. He probably had houses all over LA. Or maybe he was at Shiva's house. The thought made me want to punch a hole in Judy's door. My pickup didn't deserve that. She'd been loyal to me for years.

"Get your shit together, Cecily," I muttered as I got into the pickup and headed to Malibu.

Having my shit together was going to be imperative. I had no clue how imperative, but I was about to find out.

CHAPTER EIGHTEEN

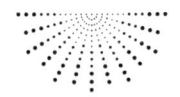

Outside the restaurant, I gripped Judy's steering wheel and debated not going through with dinner. There were paparazzi everywhere. It made me itchy. I had no clue who was at the restaurant to cause such a fuss. I was tempted to text Slash and make up a lie to get out of it, but I'd just have to reschedule. Slash might be lacking in the brains department, but my ex-husband was persistent. Plus, I didn't break promises even if they were disgusting.

"Nothing to worry about." I checked my reflection in the rearview mirror and gave myself a pep talk. "They're not here for you, Cecily Bloom. You can slip in under the radar, eat some sushi, listen to Slash's bullshit and be done with it."

While acting made me feel whole and I adored it, I'd never loved the crap that went with it. Being famous came at a high price. The loss of privacy was the worst. Not that I was all that famous, but if the show went according to plan, the vultures would come crawling out of the woodwork.

"Smile and walk fast," I told myself as I got out of the truck.

Lowering my chin, I walked like I was living in New York City—quickly and with purpose.

The flashes from the cameras were blinding. Two aggressive jerks with pornstaches blocked my entrance to the restaurant. I looked around to see who in the hell had shown up. No one had shown up. I found it very difficult to believe they were here for me.

"Cecily," someone yelled from behind me. "This way! Show us that beautiful smile, babe."

I was not his *babe*. But what I didn't want was to be on the front page of the tabloids with a surly expression. Keeping my eye roll in check, I turned and gave the turds what they wanted.

"Is it true that you and Slash are back together?" another leach shouted.

My smile felt brittle on my face. I was going to skin Slash alive when I made it into the restaurant. He'd obviously called the vultures with a tip on our fictional new relationship status.

"Nope," I said in a pleasant tone. "We're just old friends."

"Not what Slash said," another yelled and punctuated it with a lewd laugh.

Slash was so dead.

"Well, as you all *know*... Slash is prone to hallucinations," I said with a laugh so it wasn't clear if I was joking or serious.

The crowd went nuts. I was about to break out in hives.

"When's the new show airing?" Pornstache Number One yelled.

"January," I said with a real smile. "If you'll excuse me, gentlemen—and I use the term lightly—I have places to be and things to do."

"Like banging your ex?" an imbecile inquired with a suggestive smirk.

THE EDGE OF EVIL

It made me wonder if he was a Demon. I squinted at him. No glow. He was just an everyday asshole, not an Immortal one. I wanted to remove his head anyway, but revealing my own Demon status would ruin me.

Instead, I turned a homicidal glare on the man. "I'm sorry, what did you just say?" I asked icily.

The jerk backed away with an oily chuckle. However, there was always another jerk in the tabloid cesspool to step up to the plate.

"Slash said you'll be doing the beast with two backs with him later tonight," Pornstache Number Two informed me with a wink.

Slash was going down. I shrugged and fake-winced. "Actually, that's impossible. Slash has erectile dysfunction. Hasn't been able to get it up for a decade."

"Holy shit," someone from the back bellowed. "Thanks for the scoop."

I smiled and waved. "Welcome."

Literally sprinting into the restaurant, I scanned the tables for the liar. The restaurant was packed. I spotted a few Oscar winners and an overabundance of reality stars. I hated scenes like this. They weren't my speed. The bar was on the back patio. My guess was that he was out there tying one on. Getting through the crowd was going to be tricky. Being pissed off, I didn't want to have to make polite chit-chat with anyone.

Handing Slash his ass then leaving was the plan. Doing the beast with two backs wasn't part of the deal. Where the hell was the asshole?

"Babe, your outfit would look great on my bedroom floor," Slash whispered in my ear from behind. He put his arms around me and ground his pitiful erection into my backside.

My elbow was a useful body part. I wound it up, threw it back hard and knocked the wind right out of him. If I'd been thinking clearly, I would have aimed lower.

"What did you tell the leaches out there?" I hissed.

Due to the fact that Slash was a washed-up rock star and I was currently known as a former child star, our conversation barely registered to the people nearby. We weren't cool enough and that suited me just fine.

My ex was doubled over and trying to catch his breath. "I told them the truth, babe. You and me forever. Didn't know you were into the rough stuff. Me likey."

"Me no likey," I snapped. "Let's get this straight right now. This is not a date. It's an obligation on my part. I do *not* want to sleep with you. Ever. It's not happening."

Slash stood up. The grin on his face was so wide I was tempted to slap it off. "Playing hard to get is hot, babe. With school, I always wanted to get an A. With you, I just wanna F."

"You're a pig."

"Are you a drill sergeant?" he asked with a smirk, pointing to the gross bulge in his pants. "Because you have my cock standing at attention."

"Let me help you with that," I said with a smile.

The idiot thought he'd won. He was incorrect.

Kneeing him in the nards wasn't my finest moment, but it felt fabulous. As the rock star writhed on the floor, I squatted down and got in his face.

"Slash, you're an asshole. I never should have married you. You have the maturity level of a fourth-grade boy. Your dick isn't big and you're not that great in the sack. If I never see your sorry ass again, it will be too soon. And if you ever insinuate that we're together to the press again, I will sue you and I will own you," I ground out, using Cher's line to Abaddon from earlier today. It was a good one. "I'm going to the bar to have a drink. Alone. The dinner is over. Have a terrific life and thanks for the passes."

As I made my way to the bar, I heard him yell that he'd call me. Braindead didn't even begin to describe him.

This had been one of the worst days of my life. One glass of merlot was needed to calm down. I was surprised I wasn't escorted out after I'd racked a rock star, but this was LA. Everyone got racked on the regular whether it be literal or metaphorical.

"That was badass, my liege," Fifi whispered in my ear as I made my way out of the dining area and outside to the bar.

I had to slap my hand over my mouth to keep from screaming. My self-proclaimed bodyguard had to stop sneaking up on me or I was going to have a nervous breakdown.

"What are you doing here?" I demanded. My heart raced as if I'd just run a marathon.

"Protecting you," she replied, looking crestfallen at the tone of my voice.

I put my hand on her shoulder. "Thank you, but as you can see, I can protect myself."

She nodded sheepishly. I felt awful. Fifi was a sweet gal in a psychotic, grenade-carrying way.

I sighed. After the altercation between my knee and Slash's nuts, it was comforting to see a friend. "You wanna have a drink with me? My treat."

The Succubus smiled. "I would be most honored, my liege."

"Great," I said, steering us toward the bar. A horrible thought occurred. "Are you carrying grenades?"

"But of course, would you like one?" she asked as if we were speaking about something as mundane as the weather.

"Umm... no, and I don't want you using one here."

"No problem, my liege," she said with a small salute. "I'll use knives if necessary."

"Hopefully, it won't be necessary," I said with a sigh. It was a violent world I'd entered and it didn't seem like there was any going back.

I paused our forward motion and looked at my crazy new friend. "Where did you stay last night?"

"Ophelia's," she told me with a shudder. "She's a very messy person and she snores. I'm looking into buying the house next door to yours."

"It's for sale?" I asked. I hadn't noticed a sign.

"No, but money talks," she said with a grin.

I inhaled and knew I'd probably live to regret what was about to come out of my mouth, but went for it anyway. "I have a guest room. You can stay there if you don't mind bunking with Uncle Joe. I'm not even sure if he sleeps."

"I'm very impressed with Uncle Joe. I've never been ambushed by testicles until today. It was brilliantly foul. I'm considering asking him to be my mentor. He's an adorable man, wrinkled ball sac and all. If he doesn't mind my presence, I would be delighted to take my liege up on the kind offer."

"I'm pretty sure he'll be fine with it, but we can ask when we get home."

My date was over officially, and I had a new housemate who made a damn good drinking buddy when she wasn't trying to blow shit to pieces. The night was finally looking up.

And that's, of course, when everything went terribly wrong.

The view from the outdoor bar was pristine white sand and the Pacific Ocean. There were a few tables scattered on the beach for the guests. They were all empty. Surprisingly, the bar wasn't crowded. Maybe it wasn't so surprising. A crowd had formed around Slash and emptied the patio area. However, it wasn't completely deserted.

My stalker was here with his gal pal by his side.

My skin felt hot and the flush quickly rose to my cheeks. The invasion of my privacy was one thing. The throwing of the new bang-buddy in my face was vicious. Shiva wore what I could only describe as a low-cut hooker dress. She was stunning even in the tasteless and tiny piece of material barely covering her body. She sipped seductively on a Bloody Mary. It was appropriate considering I wanted to head butt her— Bloody Shiva had a lovely ring to it. For the most part, Abaddon wasn't paying her much attention, but the message he was sending me was crystal clear. He'd moved on in a nuclear option way.

"Unbelievable," I muttered under my breath. Having a beer at home with Fifi, Sean and Man-mom was the new game plan.

"Would you like to sit with Abaddon or not?" Fifi asked.

"Not," I ground out, shoving my hands into the pockets of my dress because they were about to ignite.

The Succubus frowned. "I thought you knew he was here."

"You thought wrong."

Fifi tensed up. "Shall I shank them for you, my liege? It would give me great pleasure."

For an unhinged second, I almost took her up on it. My new tendency to jump right to violence was bad. I was losing myself. My lips compressed into a thin line. I now understood Abaddon's need to put his fist through a wall. Although, planting my fist in his face would be far more satisfying. Pressing the bridge of my nose, I swallowed back the need to sob. What the hell was happening to me? I wasn't a violent person… but I was fast becoming one. I'd lopped off a few heads recently, I'd stabbed Abaddon, and I'd racked Slash.

Something Lilith had said came back to me—*Anger is healthy unless it consumes you.* I might not want a mother-daughter relationship with the woman, but her words were wise. Abaddon would not consume me. Uncle Joe had been correct, too. There was indeed a thin line between love and hate. I was now leaning hard into the hate camp.

"No shanking," I said. "But I'd rather chew broken glass than spend time with him. Let's get out of here."

"As you wish," she replied.

Exiting the way we'd arrived was impossible. The restaurant was crowded. Part of me was tempted to poof, but that wasn't smart. Even though there weren't as many people outside, there were some. While I was still unclear of the rules, it made sense not to freak humans out with magic.

"The beach," Fifi said. "We can go to the beach then around the building to the parking lot."

I nodded and started moving. From the corner of my eye, I noticed Abaddon rise to his feet and follow. Shiva pouted and tried to grab his arm. He shoved her away. The exchange was stupidly satisfying. However, the reality was that I was stupid—satisfied and seriously stupid. What they did or didn't do wasn't my business.

"Faster," I insisted, glad I'd worn flats. I had nothing to say to Abaddon and I didn't want to hear anything he had to say to me. At work, I'd deal with him. In life, I would not.

We hit the beach at a quick clip. I was relieved that Fifi hadn't thrown me over her shoulder like she'd done at the Golden Showers Bet and Bed. That would have been mortifying.

"Crap," I muttered as the ringtone for Man-mom blasted in my purse.

He knew where I was. My dad had no reason to call unless

there was an emergency. My stomach tightened and I pulled Fifi to a stop.

"I have to get this. It's my dad," I told her as I spied Abaddon catching up. "Keep him away from me, please. I'll deal with him after I talk to Man-mom."

"Your wish is my command, my liege," Fifi said, retrieving a grenade and a dagger from her jacket.

Pulling my phone out of my bag, I touched her arm. "Do not kill or maim him."

The Succubus looked disappointed, but nodded curtly before moving quickly to cut the Demon off.

"Dad?" I said, worried. "Are you okay?"

The voice on the other end of the line was not my father's. I felt dizzy and dropped to my knees in the sand. Fifi and Abaddon were in a physical altercation only ten feet away. I barely noticed.

"Who is this?" I ground out even though I recognized the voice.

She was supposed to be in time-out. My dad and brother were supposed to be safe.

"I'm your worst nightmare, Cecily Bloom," Pandora purred with a laugh so vile it made me sick.

"You're in time-out," I snapped, hoping she was playing some kind of fucked-up trick on me by cloning my dad's phone number. "You won't be my nightmare for a decade."

Fifi had not been able to stop Abaddon. They were both bloody and banged up as they stood on either side of me.

"Your father is such a handsome man," Pandora said in a seductive tone, ignoring what I'd just said.

No. This wasn't happening. Not Man-mom. He was safe. I'd kept him safe. Hadn't I? My body shook violently. I dropped my phone. Abaddon picked it up and put it on speaker.

"I understand why Lilith was so taken with him. I think we'll have so much fun together," she purred over the tiny speaker.

Abaddon's eyes turned blood red with fury, but he didn't make a sound. He pointed at Fifi to stay quiet then squatted down next to me. He held the phone close enough for me to be heard when I spoke.

"You're a liar," I ground out.

"Thank you," she replied coldly. "Normally, yes, but not today."

My eyes filled with tears. I swiped them away with my forearm. She had to be lying.

"Prove it," I said, keeping my tone as even as I could when all I wanted to do was scream. "Let me talk to him."

"As you wish," she said with an unhinged laugh.

"Cecily?" my dad asked, sounding like he hadn't slept in weeks.

I dug my flaming hands into the sand so I didn't blow up the entirety of Malibu.

"Dad, it's me," I said shakily. "Are you okay?"

The question was absurd. He was obviously not okay.

"I'm okay, Cecily-boo. Don't come after me. That's what she wants."

Pandora's hysterical laughter in the background made my skin crawl.

Man-mom continued, sounding weaker with each word. "I'm an old man. I've lived a wonderful life. Remember when I told you I would step in front of a train to save you or Sean?"

"I do," I whispered as tears rolled down my cheeks.

"The train has arrived," he said softly. "I meant it then and I mean it now. I love you, Cecily-boo, and I always will."

I could hear the smile in his voice. It made me cry harder.

How was this happening? How did the scum of the Universe break out of Demon jail?

"Wasn't that sweet?" Pandora snarled, back on the line. "Would you like to make a deal, *Cecily-boo*?"

My nickname on her lips was horrendous. "What are the terms?"

Abaddon shook his head. I put my hand up to let him know this was my problem and he wasn't involved.

"Your life for your father's," she said gleefully. "Even trade, little Goddess. No stress, no mess."

I sucked back my tears. I was a badass. Badasses took care of their own. "Where and when?"

"That's for me to know and you to figure out," she hissed. "And you'd better figure it out quick. Daddy Dearest has three days before he breathes no more. Good luck, Cecily-boo. You will need it."

The call went dead as my panic attack roared to life. My vision blurred and my head felt like it was going to explode. Getting air into my lungs was painful and difficult. My dad was one of the most precious people in my life. His love for me and mine for him was the most real and unconditional love I'd known.

The arms around me were strong and comforting. The words whispered in my ear were calming. I rested my head on a strong chest. Slowly, my breathing became normal. Slowly, the pain in my head receded. Slowly, my vision cleared.

I knew who held me. It felt so incredibly right even though it was tragically wrong. God, how I wanted it to be different.

As soon as it was clear that I was okay, the Demon abruptly let me go and moved away. I felt the loss acutely. That was my problem. Not his. I'd get over it. I stood up and took a deep breath.

Maybe, Abaddon would help me. He'd had a longtime friendship with my father. He might despise me, but it was impossible to hate Bill Bloom.

I steeled myself to feel nothing and looked right into Abaddon's eyes. "I need your help."

Shiva's hiss of displeasure from behind him made me see red. Without thinking, I raised my hand and electrocuted the living daylights out of her. I was lucky no humans were around to witness it. Her furious shouts were enjoyable. I wiggled my fingers and doused the flames that covered her. I also dressed her in a burlap sack.

"I've had enough, Sheba. One more shitty word out of you and you'll be bald and sporting facial hair. I'm not encroaching on your territory. Your lover will be home to you soon."

Abaddon looked at me as if I'd lost my mind. I had, but not about this.

"I am not—" he started.

My hand shot up. The Demon had a lot more to say, evidenced by his incredulous expression. All I needed was the answer to my question. "Don't care and don't want to know. All I need to know is if you'll help me find my dad."

"You're an idiot, Cecily," he said.

"Correct. Is that your answer? Because if it is, I'll move on to someone else."

His eyes narrowed. "Thought you already did." His voice was flat, but his red eyes showed his ire.

I didn't have time for games. He was not the one for me, and I was not the one for him. It had been a mistake to ask for his help. I had Lilith's number memorized. I would call her. I knew in my heart she was as invested in my dad's safety as I was. And while she couldn't engage directly with Pandora, I could.

And I would.

I glanced over at Fifi, who was holding a grenade in each hand, ready to lob it at Abaddon or Shiva. "We're out," I told her.

"No, you're not," Abaddon snapped, grabbing my hands and holding them in a vise-like grip. "I'll help you."

"Are you being honest?" I asked. "I can't have your hatred for me getting in the way of saving my dad."

The Demon was pissed. His eyes literally shot red sparks. "Again, you're an idiot."

"Already established," I said. "I need your word that you'll put aside your feelings and be loyal to me for the next few days."

He laughed. I didn't get the joke.

"You have my word, Goddess Cecily," he replied with the barest hint of a smile on his lips.

I nodded. "Fifi, let the others know what happened and make sure Sean is okay. Protect my brother with your life."

"On it," she replied, vanishing in a bright and glittery rose-colored mist.

"Shiva," I said, looking at the soaking-wet, burlap-covered Demon. "You will alert Lilith. Immediately."

"Yes, Goddess Cecily," she replied woodenly before she poofed away.

I didn't trust her, but Abaddon and Lilith did. I'd have to give a little.

"Are you ready?" Abaddon asked with an expression I couldn't decipher.

The question seemed loaded but I took it at face value. "Where are we going?"

His head tilted to the side, and he stared at my lips for a moment. "To the Darkness."

I closed my eyes and tried to find the serene feeling I'd experienced with Uncle Joe after our yoga session. It was nowhere to be found.

"Take me to Hell, Demon," I said.

His beauty was stupid. His smile held secrets. "If we go, there may be no coming back."

Again, I knew he was saying much more than his words implied. Again, it didn't matter. All that mattered was bringing Man-mom safely home. Period.

"Take me anyway," I said.

"*Nothing* would give me more pleasure."

In a blast of shimmering black magic, we left Malibu.

I had no clue what was coming next, but I'd cried my river of tears and built a bridge to get over it. I would cross it as a badass and maybe even live to tell.

The train had not arrived to take my dad.

Pandora was not the train.

I was the train, and I was going to tie her to the tracks and run her over until she was unrecognizable even to herself.

Time to get the party started.

The End… for now

Want to read the next book in the series?? Go HERE to buy The Bold and the Banished now!

NEXT IN THE GOOD TO THE LAST DEMON SERIES

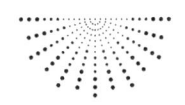

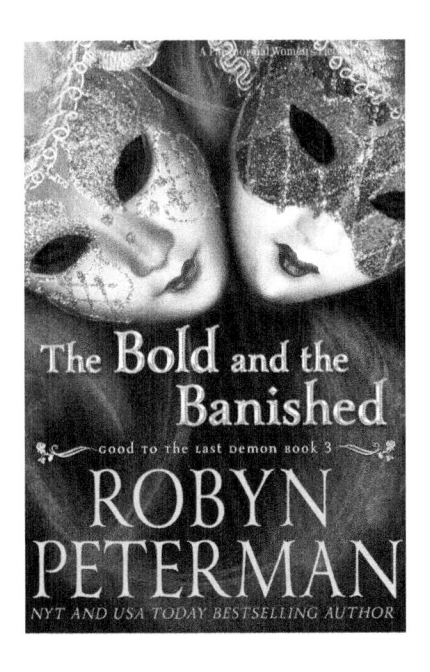

My motto—Let's get this party started. My goal—staying alive.

Recently, I was given my own sitcom and my forties were looking fabulous. My dreams were finally coming true—*were* being the operative word.

Of course, just when I think I might have a grip on my newly discovered Demon status, it all goes to Hell. Literally.

I've gone from enemies-to-lovers back to enemies with the hottest Demon alive, who also happens to be the producer on my show. What I'd like to do is never see Abaddon's stupidly handsome face again.

Too bad, so sad. I need his help. The evil whack-job Pandora has kidnapped someone who I love and adore. That's not working for me. At all.

With a grenade carrying Succubus, an Angel with a penchant for blue lipliner, a Demon with bigger boobs than sense, and Abaddon on my team, I'm going into the Darkness to save someone I can't live without.

I have no clue what's coming next, but as an actress I'm not afraid to go method. I've already cried my river of tears and built a bridge to get over it. I'll cross it as a badass as I face my Immortal enemy, because in my line of work, fortune favors the Bold.

ORDER THE BOLD AND THE BANISHED NOW!!

EXCERPT: THE WRITE HOOK

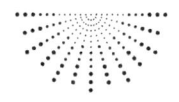

BOOK DESCRIPTION

THE WRITE HOOK

Midlife is full of surprises. Not all of them are working for me.

At forty-two I've had my share of ups and downs. Relatively normal, except when the definition of normal changes… drastically.

NYT Bestselling Romance Author: Check
Amazing besties: Check
Lovely home: Check
Pet cat named Thick Stella who wants to kill me: Check
Wacky Tabacky Dealing Aunt: Check
Cheating husband banging the weather girl on our kitchen table: Check
Nasty Divorce: Oh yes
Characters from my novels coming to life: Umm… yes
Crazy: Possibly

Four months of wallowing in embarrassed depression should

BOOK DESCRIPTION

be enough. I'm beginning to realize that no one is who they seem to be, and my life story might be spinning out of my control. It's time to take a shower, put on a bra, and wear something other than sweatpants. Difficult, but doable.

With my friends—real and imaginary—by my side, I need to edit my life before the elusive darkness comes for all of us.

The plot is no longer fiction. It's my reality, and I'm writing a happy ever after no matter what. I just have to find the *write hook*.

CHAPTER 1

"I didn't leave that bowl in the sink," I muttered to no one as I stared in confusion at the blue piece of pottery with milk residue in the bottom. "Wait. Did I?"

Slowly backing away, I ran my hands through my hair that hadn't seen a brush in days—possibly longer—and decided that I wasn't going to think too hard about it. Thinking led to introspective thought, which led to dealing with reality, and that was a no-no.

Reality wasn't my thing right now.

Maybe I'd walked in my sleep, eaten a bowl of cereal, then politely put the bowl in the sink. It was possible.

"That has to be it," I announced, walking out of the kitchen and avoiding all mirrors and any glass where I could catch a glimpse of myself.

It was time to get to work. Sadly, books didn't write themselves.

"I can do this. I have to do this." I sat down at my desk and made sure my posture didn't suck. I was fully aware it would suck in approximately five minutes, but I wanted to start out

CHAPTER 1

right. It would be a bad week to throw my back out. "Today, I'll write ten thousand words. They will be coherent. I will not mistakenly or on purpose make a list of the plethora of ways I would like to kill Darren. He's my past. Beheading him is illegal. I'm far better than that. On a more positive note, my imaginary muse will show his ponytailed, obnoxious ass up today, and I won't play Candy Jelly Crush until the words are on the page."

Two hours later...

Zero words. However, I'd done three loads of laundry—sweatpants, t-shirts and underwear—and played Candy Jelly Crush until I didn't have any more lives. As pathetic as I'd become, I hadn't sunk so low as to purchase new lives. That would mean I'd hit rock bottom. Of course, I was precariously close, evidenced by my cussing out of the Jelly Queen for ten minutes, but I didn't pay for lives. I considered it a win.

I'd planned on folding the laundry but decided to vacuum instead. I'd fold the loads by Friday. It was Tuesday. That was reasonable. If they were too wrinkled, I'd simply wash them again. No biggie. After the vacuuming was done, I rearranged my office for thirty minutes. I wasn't sure how to Feng Shui, but after looking it up on my phone, I gave it a half-assed effort.

Glancing around at my handiwork, I nodded. "Much better. If the surroundings are aligned correctly, the words will flow magically. I hope."

Two hours later...

"Mother humper," I grunted as I pushed my monstrosity of a bed from one side of the bedroom to the other. "This weighs a damn ton."

I'd burned all the bedding seven weeks ago. The bonfire had been cathartic. I'd taken pictures as the five hundred

CHAPTER 1

thread count sheets had gone up in flame. I'd kept the comforter. I'd paid a fortune for it. It had been thoroughly saged and washed five times. Even though there was no trace of Darren left in the bedroom, I'd been sleeping in my office.

The house was huge, beautiful... and mine—a gorgeously restored Victorian where I'd spent tons of time as a child. It had an enchanted feel to it that I adored. I didn't need such an enormous abode, but I loved the location—the middle of nowhere. The internet was iffy, but I solved that by going into town to the local coffee shop if I had something important to download or send.

Darren, with the wandering pecker, thought he would get a piece of the house. He was wrong. I'd inherited it from my whackadoo grandmother and great-aunt Flip. My parents hadn't always been too keen on me spending so much time with Granny and Aunt Flip growing up, but I adored the two old gals so much they'd relented. Since I spent a lot of time in an imaginary dream world, my mom and dad were delighted when I related to actual people—even if they were left of center.

Granny and Flip made sure the house was in my name only—nontransferable and non-sellable. It was stipulated that I had to pass it to a family member or the Historical Society when I died. Basically, I had life rights. It was as if Granny and Aunt Flip had known I would waste two decades of my life married to a jackhole who couldn't keep his salami in his pants and would need someplace to live. God rest Granny's insane soul. Aunt Flip was still kicking, although I hadn't seen her in a few years.

Aunt Flip put the K in kooky. She'd bought a cottage in the hills about an hour away and grew medicinal marijuana—before it was legal. The old gal was the black sheep of the

CHAPTER 1

family and preferred her solitude and her pot to company. She hadn't liked Darren a bit. She and Granny both had worn black to my wedding. Everyone had been appalled—even me—but in the end, it made perfect sense. I had to hand it to the old broads. They'd been smarter than me by a long shot. And the house? It had always been my charmed haven in the storm.

Even though there were four spare bedrooms plus the master suite, I chose my office. It felt safe to me.

Thick Stella preferred my office, and I needed to be around something that had a heartbeat. It didn't matter that Thick Stella was bitchy and swiped at me with her deadly kitty claws every time I passed her. I loved her. The feeling didn't seem mutual, but she hadn't left me for a twenty-three-year-old with silicone breast implants and huge, bright white teeth.

"Thick Stella, do you think Sasha should wear red to her stepmother's funeral?" I asked as I plopped down on my newly Feng Shuied couch and narrowly missed getting gouged by my cat. "Yes or no? Hiss at me if it's a yes. Growl at me if it's a no."

Thick Stella had a go at her privates. She was useless.

"That wasn't an answer." I grabbed my laptop from my desk. Deciding it was too dangerous to sit near my cat, I settled for the love seat. The irony of the piece of furniture I'd chosen didn't escape me.

"I think she should wear red," I told Thick Stella, who didn't give a crap what Sasha wore. "Her stepmother was an asshat, and it would show fabu disrespect."

Typing felt good. Getting lost in a story felt great. I dressed Sasha in a red Prada sheath, then had her behead her ex-husband with a dull butter knife when he and his bimbo showed up unexpectedly to pay their respects at the funeral home. It was a bloodbath. Putting Sasha in red was an excellent move. The blood matched her frock to a T.

CHAPTER 1

Quickly rethinking the necessary murder, I moved the scene of the decapitation to the empty lobby of the funeral home. It would suck if I had to send Sasha to prison. She hadn't banged Damien yet, and everyone was eagerly awaiting the sexy buildup—including me. It was the fourth book in the series, and it was about time they got together. The sexual tension was palpable.

"What in the freaking hell?" I snapped my laptop shut and groaned. "Sasha doesn't have an ex-husband. I can't do this. I've got nothing." Where was my muse hiding? I needed the elusive imaginary idiot if I was going to get any writing done. "Chauncey, dammit, where are you?"

"My God, you're loud, Clementine," a busty, beautiful woman dressed in a deep purple Regency gown said with an eye roll.

She was seated on the couch next to Thick Stella, who barely acknowledged her. My cat attacked strangers and friends. Not today. My fat feline simply glanced over at the intruder and yawned. The cat was a traitor.

Forget the furry betrayer. How in the heck did the woman get into my house—not to mention my office—without me seeing her enter? For a brief moment, I wondered if she'd banged my husband too but pushed the sordid thought out of my head. She looked to be close to thirty—too old for the asshole.

"Who are you?" I demanded, holding my laptop over my head as a weapon.

If I threw it and it shattered, I would be screwed. I couldn't remember the last time I'd backed it up. If I lost the measly, somewhat disjointed fifty thousand words I'd written so far, I'd have to start over. That wouldn't fly with my agent or my publisher.

CHAPTER 1

"Don't be daft," the woman replied. "It's rather unbecoming. May I ask a question?"

"No, you may not," I shot back, trying to place her.

She was clearly a nutjob. The woman was rolling up on thirty but had the vernacular of a seventy-year-old British society matron. She was dressed like she'd walked off the set of a film starring Emma Thompson. Her blonde hair shone to the point of absurdity and was twisted into an elaborate up-do. Wispy tendrils framed her perfectly heart-shaped face. Her sparkling eyes were lavender, enhanced by the over-the-top gown she wore.

Strangely, she was vaguely familiar. I just couldn't remember how I knew her.

"How long has it been since you attended to your hygiene?" she inquired.

Putting my laptop down and picking up a lamp, I eyed her. I didn't care much for the lamp or her question. I had been thinking about Marie Condo-ing my life, and the lamp didn't bring me all that much joy. If it met its demise by use of self-defense, so be it. "I don't see how that's any of your business, lady. What I'd suggest is that you leave. Now. Or else I'll call the police. Breaking and entering is a crime."

She laughed. It sounded like freaking bells. Even though she was either a criminal or certifiable, she was incredibly charming.

"Oh dear," she said, placing her hand delicately on her still heaving, milky-white bosom. "You are so silly. The constable knows quite well that I'm here. He advised me to come."

"The constable?" I asked, wondering how far off her rocker she was.

She nodded coyly. "Most certainly. We're all terribly concerned."

CHAPTER 1

I squinted at her. "About my hygiene?"

"That, amongst other things," she confirmed. "Darling girl, you are not an ace of spades or, heaven forbid, an adventuress. Unless you want to be an ape leader, I'd recommend bathing."

"Are you right in the head?" I asked, wondering where I'd left my damn cell phone. It was probably in the laundry room. I was going to be murdered by a nutjob, and I'd lost my chance to save myself because I'd been playing Candy Jelly Crush. The headline would be horrifying—*Homeless-looking, Hygiene-free Paranormal Romance Author Beheaded by Victorian Psycho.*

If I lived through the next hour, I was deleting the game for good.

"I think it would do wonders for your spirit if you donned a nice tight corset and a clean chemise," she suggested, skillfully ignoring my question. "You must pull yourself together. Your behavior is dicked in the nob."

I sat down and studied her. My about-to-be-murdered radar relaxed a tiny bit, but I kept the lamp clutched tightly in my hand. My gut told me she wasn't going to strangle me. Of course, I could be mistaken, but Purple Gal didn't seem violent —just bizarre. Plus, the lamp was heavy. I could knock her ladylike ass out with one good swing.

How in the heck did I know her? College? Grad School? The grocery store? At forty-two, I'd met a lot of people in my life. Was she with the local community theater troop? I was eighty-six percent sure she wasn't here to off me. However, I'd been wrong about life-altering events before—like not knowing my husband was boffing someone young enough to have been our daughter.

"What language are you speaking?" I spotted a pair of scissors on my desk. If I needed them, it was a quick move to grab

CHAPTER 1

them. I'd never actually killed anyone except in fictitious situations, but there was a first time for everything.

Pulling an embroidered lavender hankey from her cleavage, she clutched it and twisted it in her slim fingers. "Clementine, *you* should know."

"I'm at a little disadvantage here," I said, fascinated by the batshit crazy woman who'd broken into my home. "You seem to know my name, but I don't know yours."

And that was when the tears started. Hers. Not mine.

"Such claptrap. How very unkind of you, Clementine," she burst out through her stupidly attractive sobs.

It was ridiculous how good the woman looked while crying. I got all blotchy and red, but not the mystery gal in purple. She grew even more lovely. It wasn't fair. I still had no clue what the hell she was talking about, but on the off chance she might throw a tantrum if I asked more questions, I kept my mouth shut.

And yes, she had a point, but my *hygiene* was none of her damn business. I couldn't quite put my finger on the last time I'd showered. If I had to guess, it was probably in the last five to twelve days. I was on a deadline for a book. To be more precise, I was late for my deadline on a book. I didn't exactly have time for personal sanitation right now.

And speaking of deadlines...

"How about this?" My tone was excessively polite. I almost laughed. The woman had illegally entered my house, and I was behaving like she was a guest. "I'll take a shower later today after I get through a few pivotal chapters. Right now, you should leave so I can work."

"Yes, of course," she replied, absently stroking Fat Stella, who purred. If I'd done that, I would be minus a finger. "It would be dreadfully sad if you were under the hatches."

CHAPTER 1

I nodded. "Right. That would, umm... suck."

The woman in purple smiled. It was radiant, and I would have sworn I heard birds happily chirping. I was losing it.

"Excellent," she said, pulling a small periwinkle velvet bag from her cleavage. I wondered what else she had stored in there and hoped there wasn't a weapon. "I shall leave you with two gold coins. While the Grape Nuts were tasty, I would prefer that you purchase some Lucky Charms. I understand they are magically delicious."

"It was you?" I asked, wildly relieved that I hadn't been sleep eating. I had enough problems at the moment. Gaining weight from midnight dates with cereal wasn't on the to-do list.

"It was," she confirmed, getting to her feet and dropping the coins into my hand. "The consistency was quite different from porridge, but I found it tasty—very crunchy."

"Right... well... thank you for putting the bowl in the sink." Wait. Why the hell was I thanking her? She'd wandered in and eaten my Grape Nuts.

"You are most welcome, Clementine," she said with a disarming smile that lit up her unusual eyes. "It was lovely finally meeting you even if your disheveled outward show is entirely astonishing."

I was reasonably sure I had just been insulted by the cereal lover, but it was presented with excellent manners. However, she did answer a question. We hadn't met. I wasn't sure why she seemed familiar. The fact that she knew my name was alarming.

"Are you a stalker?" I asked before I could stop myself.

I'd had a few over the years. Being a *New York Times* bestselling author was something I was proud of, but it had come with a little baggage here and there. Some people seemed to

CHAPTER 1

have difficulty discerning fiction from reality. If I had to guess, I'd say Purple Gal might be one of those people.

I'd only written one Regency novel, and that had been at the beginning of my career, before I'd found my groove in paranormal romance. I was way more comfortable writing about demons and vampires than people dressed in top hats and hoopskirts. Maybe the crazy woman had read my first book. It hadn't done well, and for good reason. It was over-the-top bad. I'd blocked the entire novel out of my mind. Live and learn. It had been my homage to Elizabeth Hoyt well over a decade ago. It had been clear to all that I should leave Regency romance to the masters.

"Don't be a Merry Andrew," the woman chided me. "Your bone box is addled. We must see to it at once. I shall pay a visit again soon."

The only part of her gibberish I understood was that she thought she was coming back. Note to self—change all the locks on the doors. Since it wasn't clear if she was packing heat in her cleavage, I just smiled and nodded.

"Alrighty then..." I was unsure if I should walk her to the door or if she would let herself out. Deciding it would be better to make sure she actually left instead of letting her hide in my pantry to finish off my cereal, I gestured to the door. "Follow me."

Thick Stella growled at me. I was so tempted to flip her off but thought it might earn another lecture from Purple Gal. It was more than enough to be lambasted for my appearance. I didn't need my manners picked apart by someone with a tenuous grip on reality.

My own grip was dubious as it was.

"You might want to reconsider breaking into homes," I said, holding the front door open. "It could end badly—for you."

CHAPTER 1

Part of me couldn't believe that I was trying to help the nutty woman out, but I couldn't seem to stop myself. I kind of liked her.

"I'll keep that in mind," she replied as she sauntered out of my house into the warm spring afternoon. "Remember, Clementine, there is always sunshine after the rain."

As she made her way down the long sunlit, tree-lined drive, she didn't look back. It was disturbingly like watching the end of a period movie where the heroine left her old life behind and walked proudly toward her new and promising future.

Glancing around for a car, I didn't spot one. Had she left it parked on the road so she could make a clean getaway after she'd bludgeoned me? Had I just politely escorted a murderer out of my house?

Had I lost it for real?

Probably.

As she disappeared from sight, I felt the weight of the gold coins still clutched in my hand. Today couldn't get any stranger.

At least, I hoped not.

Opening my fist to examine the coins, I gasped. "What in the heck?"

There was nothing in my hand.

Had I dropped them? Getting down on all fours, I searched. Thick Stella joined me, kind of—more like watched me as I crawled around and wondered if anything that had just happened had actually happened.

"Purple Gal gave me coins to buy Lucky Charms," I told my cat, my search now growing frantic. "You saw her do it. Right? She sat next to you. And you didn't attack her. *Right?*"

Thick Stella simply stared at me. What did I expect? If my cat answered me, I'd have to commit myself. That option

CHAPTER 1

might still be on the table. Had I just imagined the entire exchange with the strange woman? Should I call the cops?

"And tell them what?" I asked, standing back up and locking the front door securely. "That a woman in a purple gown broke in and ate my cereal while politely insulting my hygiene? Oh, and she left me two gold coins that disappeared in my hand as soon as she was out of sight? That's not going to work."

I'd call the police if she came back, since I wasn't sure she'd been here at all. She hadn't threatened to harm me. Purple Gal had been charming and well-mannered the entire time she'd badmouthed my cleanliness habits. And to be quite honest, real or not, she'd made a solid point. I could use a shower.

Maybe four months of wallowing in self-pity and only living inside the fictional worlds I created on paper had taken more of a toll than I was aware of. Getting lost in my stories was one of my favorite things to do. It had saved me more than once over the years. It was possible that I'd let it go too far. Hence, the Purple Gal hallucination.

Shit.

First things first. Delete Candy Jelly Crush. Getting rid of the white noise in my life was the first step to... well, the first step to something.

I'd figure it out later.

HIT HERE TO ORDER THE WRITE HOOK!!!!!

ROBYN'S BOOK LIST

(IN CORRECT READING ORDER)

HOT DAMNED SERIES
Fashionably Dead
Fashionably Dead Down Under
Hell on Heels
Fashionably Dead in Diapers
A Fashionably Dead Christmas
Fashionably Hotter Than Hell
Fashionably Dead and Wed
Fashionably Fanged
Fashionably Flawed
A Fashionably Dead Diary
Fashionably Forever After
Fashionably Fabulous
A Fashionable Fiasco
Fashionably Fooled
Fashionably Dead and Loving It
Fashionably Dead and Demonic
The Oh My Gawd Couple
A Fashionable Disaster

GOOD TO THE LAST DEMON SERIES
As the Underworld Turns
The Edge of Evil
The Bold and the Banished

GOOD TO THE LAST DEATH SERIES
It's a Wonderful Midlife Crisis
Whose Midlife Crisis Is It Anyway?
A Most Excellent Midlife Crisis
My Midlife Crisis, My Rules
You Light Up My Midlife Crisis
It's A Matter of Midlife and Death
The Facts Of Midlife
It's A Hard Knock Midlife
Run for Your Midlife

MY SO-CALLED MYSTICAL MIDLIFE SERIES
The Write Hook
You May Be Write
All The Write Moves
My Big Fat Hairy Wedding

SHIFT HAPPENS SERIES
Ready to Were
Some Were in Time
No Were To Run
Were Me Out
Were We Belong

MAGIC AND MAYHEM SERIES
Switching Hour
Witch Glitch

ROBYN'S BOOK LIST

A Witch in Time
Magically Delicious
A Tale of Two Witches
Three's A Charm
Switching Witches
You're Broom or Mine?
The Bad Boys of Assjacket
The Newly Witch Game
Witches In Stitches

SEA SHENANIGANS SERIES
Tallulah's Temptation
Ariel's Antics
Misty's Mayhem
Petunia's Pandemonium
Jingle Me Balls

A WYLDE PARANORMAL SERIES
Beauty Loves the Beast

HANDCUFFS AND HAPPILY EVER AFTERS SERIES
How Hard Can it Be?
Size Matters
Cop a Feel

If after reading all the above you are still wanting more adventure and zany fun, read *Pirate Dave and His Randy Adventures*, the romance novel budding novelist Rena helped wicked Evangeline write in *How Hard Can It Be?*

Warning: Pirate Dave Contains Romance Satire, Spoofing, and Pirates with Two Pork Swords.

NOTE FROM THE AUTHOR

If you enjoyed reading *As The Edge of Evil*, please consider leaving a positive review or rating on the site where you purchased it. Reader reviews help my books continue to be valued by resellers and help new readers make decisions about reading them.

You are the reason I write these stories and I sincerely appreciate each of you!

Many thanks for your support,
~ Robyn Peterman

Want to hear about my new releases? Visit https://robynpeterman.com/newsletter/ and join my mailing list!

ABOUT ROBYN PETERMAN

Robyn Peterman writes because the people inside her head won't leave her alone until she gives them life on paper. Her addictions include laughing really hard with friends, shoes (the expensive kind), Target, Coke (the drink not the drug LOL) with extra ice in a Yeti cup, bejeweled reading glasses, her kids, her super-hot hubby and collecting stray animals.

A former professional actress with Broadway, film and T.V. credits, she now lives in the South with her family and too many animals to count.

Writing gives her peace and makes her whole, plus having a job where she can work in sweatpants works really well for her.